ASCENDANT

A.L. KNORR
MARTHA CARR

ASCENDANT

The Kacy Chronicles Book 2
By A.L. Knorr and Martha Carr

From A. L. Knorr

For anyone who ever wished they could fly.

From Martha

To everyone who still believes in magic and all the possibilities that holds.
To all the readers who make this entire ride so much fun.
And to all the dreamers just like me who create wonder, big and small, every day.

A part of
The Revelations of Oriceran Universe
Written and Created
by Michael Anderle & Martha Carr

The Oriceran Universe
(and what happens within / characters / situations / worlds) are
Copyright (c) 2017-2018 by Martha Carr and LMPBN Publishing.

ASCENDANT (this book) is a work of fiction.

All of the characters, organizations, and events portrayed in this novel are either products of the author's imagination or are used fictitiously. Sometimes both.

This book Copyright © 2017 A.L. Knorr and Martha Carr
Cover Design by Damonza
Cover copyright © LMBPN Publishing

LMBPN Publishing supports the right to free expression and the value of copyright. The purpose of copyright is to encourage writers and artists to produce the creative works that enrich our culture.

The distribution of this book without permission is a theft of the author's intellectual property. If you would like permission to use material from the book (other than for review purposes), please contact info@kurtherianbooks.com. Thank you for your support of the author's rights.

LMBPN Publishing
PMB 196, 2540 South Maryland Pkwy
Las Vegas, NV 89109

First US edition, October 2017
Version 1.03, January 2018

The Oriceran Universe (and what happens within / characters / situations / worlds) are Copyright (c) 2017-2018 by Martha Carr and LMBPN Publishing.

※ Created with Vellum

ASCENDANT TEAM

JIT BETA READERS

Kelly ODonnell
Alex Wilson
Paul Westman
Micky Cocker
Larry Omans
Kimberly Boyer
Joshua Ahles
Nicola Aquino

If we missed anyone, please let us know!

CHAPTER 1

*E*ohne lay with her back in the dirt and a cloth bag under her head to serve as a pillow. She munched on a piece of grass as she gazed at the stars sparkling down over Charra-Rae. The Arpaks—Jordan and Sol—had left that morning. Though Eohne felt a surprising amount of loss for two people she'd only just met, she figured it was probably a good thing they'd gone. Jordan had been a welcome distraction; it would be too easy to get involved in Jordan's search for her mother, too easy for Eohne to abandon her own mission—the mission Sohne had charged her with.

'Find a way to synthesize the gersher fungus,' had been Sohne's command. Eohne had documented all one hundred and seventy-three attempts. All had failed. Eohne was the Charra-Rae Elves' best inventor, best deductive mind, and supposedly the most adept—other than Sohne herself—at understanding the language at the root of their magic. Yet so far, she hadn't even come close to success. She was able to remake the fungi so that it smelled, tasted, and had texture identical to the real thing, but it had none of the healing benefits. It was an impotent forgery, a perfect likeness in every way except for the way that mattered.

A small cloud of what looked like glitter flashed through the air, drawing Eohne's eyes to the treetops at the edge of the glen. Here they came—her messenger bugs, back from their delivery to Allan, Jordan's father. Eohne reached for the jar sitting in the grass by her hip and tapped a fingernail against the glass.

Clink, clink, clink! Her messenger bugs plopped themselves into the jar as Eohne counted the sounds of their bodies hitting the glass. *Eleven, twelve, thirteen...*

The glass went quiet. Eohne frowned and sat up, looking into the starry darkness yawning overhead. She waited, but it took mere seconds of silence for her to deduce that something had gone wrong.

The messenger bugs are tethered together by magic; it is impossible for only some of them to return and not others. Isn't it?

She picked up the jar with the little glass balls nestled inside, their legs tucked away. She recounted, but it was a useless exercise. It was easy to eyeball that almost half of her bugs were missing.

She withdrew the syringe she had used to inject the bugs with Jordan's vocal vibrations, and plucked a bug from the jar. Inserting the needle into the belly of the bug, she drew out the liquid. Normally she would discard the juice—it had served its purpose and it wasn't bringing any return message. But there might be some information hidden within that would help Eohne work out what had happened.

She sprayed a small amount of the liquid into her palm and pressed her middle finger into it. She closed her eyes, shutting out the night. But there was nothing. No vibrations to pick up, no information. The liquid was dead.

She wiped the dampness away, huffed with frustration, and screwed the cap back on the jar. She got to her feet and tucked the jar into her sack. She brushed the leaves out of her hair and dusted the dirt from her clothing, and then made her way down the hill, into the forest, winding through the narrow loamy path towards home. Her footfalls were silent, her form a ghost in the woods, but her razor-sharp inventor's mind was racing. *What does this mean? What has happened to the rest of my bugs?*

The music of flutes and drums drifted through the ferns and leaves. The bright blue fire of the Charra-Rae Elves had been lit, and the smell of elvish cooking reached Eohne's nose. Her stomach rumbled, but she was too distressed to think about food. She reached the outskirts of the gathering and combed the faces for Sohne.

The copper-haired Elf wasn't difficult to spot. Sohne was talking with two of the elders and drinking from a wooden chalice, lounging in an elaborately carved wooden chair while the elders stood around her. Eohne crossed the circle and approached as Sohne and the elders burst into laughter over something.

"Do you have a moment?" Eohne asked in the tongue of Charra-Rae, her head bowed.

Sohne's laughter died away, and she turned cool eyes on the inferior Elf. "What is it?"

"May I speak with you alone, please?"

Sohne pressed her lips together but nodded to the elders. "Give us a moment."

The others moved away toward the food. Sohne got up from her seat, and the two elven women turned away from the crowd and moved towards the outskirts of the party. Eohne stayed just behind Sohne, the way she knew Sohne liked. When they were out of earshot, Eohne waited for Sohne to face her and signal that she could speak.

Keeping her eyes down, Eohne said, "I allowed Jordan to use my messenger bugs to get a message to her father."

"That was foolish," answered Sohne, crossing a long forearm over her stomach. Her voice was not disdainful, simply matter-of-fact. "Did it work?"

"Partially. Not all of them have returned."

Sohne cocked her head quizzically at Eohne. The shadows on her face sharpened in the firelight. "Where are the others?"

"That's why I came to you. This has never happened before." Eohne wilted inside as Sohne's face hardened. She forged on, forcing her voice to sound stronger than she felt. "I can only assume they remain on Earth, though I've no idea why."

"There was no information returned with them?"

"Nothing. The juice is flat. Dead."

Sohne let a long breath out through her nose. "But you don't know if it's dead because the missing bugs were destroyed somehow, or if it's dead because the rest are still trapped on Earth?"

"No." Eohne dropped her eyes to Sohne's feet. "I don't know."

"You had better hope that it's the former."

Eohne finally looked up with an expression of surprise. "Hope is not enough in this case. I need to get them back. It might have been foolish for me to send a message to Earth, but it would be even more foolish to leave them there."

A look of understanding crossed Sohne's stark and beautiful features. Her sapphire eyes glimmered in the light. "You want to know if you can leave Charra-Rae?"

"Yes."

Sohne shook her head. "Your assignment is too important. I don't want you diverting your attention from it."

"But—"

"What do you think would happen to Charra-Rae if the gersher fungus stopped producing?" Sohne asked; her tone had an edge that made Eohne cringe.

Eohne's mouth had gone dry at the denial to her request, but it didn't stop her from challenging Sohne again. "How likely is that to happen?" The fungus dying off at random was an eventuality that seemed near impossible to Eohne. It was true that it was their most important export, but they'd never suffered a serious dearth of it before—only slower growth cycles.

"We don't know, do we?" Sohne answered with a frown. "We

can't cultivate it; its magic remains elusive to you. You can replicate every other substance so perfectly that there is no discernible difference between yours and nature's. Why not the fungus?" Sohne cocked an accusatory eyebrow and crossed her arms. "If you had solved the problem already, I would be happy to let you go. But—" She shrugged in a way that said, *this is on you, not me.*

Eohne frowned at her senior. "The fungus is not in short supply. We haven't had a deficiency in over eighteen years. But if those bugs are trapped on earth somehow, we've just knowingly left someone the ability to make a new portal—"

"Not we," interrupted Sohne. "You." She dropped her arms and pointed a long finger into Eohne's chest. "This was a risk that you decided to take. Live with it." With that, the redheaded Elf turned her back on Eohne and returned to the fire. She looked back over her shoulder once to say, "Eat, Eohne. You need your strength."

Eohne turned away from the fire and walked the faintly glimmering path to her home, seething. Sohne could be a brilliant leader—she could even give the impression of having compassion, at times. But Sohne never did anything that didn't strengthen, protect, or position the Elves of Charra-Rae for a safe and secure future. What did she care if some random Earthling accidentally found his or her way through to Oriceran, or got trapped in the in-between?

Maybe Sohne didn't care, but Eohne did. Eohne cared very much.

CHAPTER 2

*J*ordan followed Sol as he descended to a large flagstone terrace. Throughout the stones in patchwork style were pockets of plants, foliage, trees, and flowers—some of which looked a lot like plants from Earth—but there was always something just a little bit different about them. There were flowers that had the droopy conical blossoms of foxglove, only with several long red pistils flowing out from each blossom and drifting in the breeze like hair.

"Where are we?" Jordan asked, closing up her wings and wandering closer to the nearest garden patch, drawn by a sweet fragrance. "I mean, I know we're in Maticaw. But whose place is this?"

She bent down to inhale, but had to go slowly. She still wasn't used to the weight of her wings, and the muscular soreness that had come with the last few days of travel was only now just starting to ease. Sol had coached her to keep her wings slightly flexed while walking—or just behaving like a biped in general—rather than letting them relax and go limp, but not before she'd toppled over more than once when bending over, as the weight of her wings pulled her forward unexpectedly. Jordan had a sneaking suspicion Sol had enjoyed her ungraceful tumbles and had delayed giving her this handy little tip.

"This is where Cles lives and works; I've come to deliver this," he held up a small folded yellow letter. "I'm not sure how long this will take. It depends on what it says and if he needs to write a reply. Do you mind waiting here?"

"Not at all." Jordan breathed in the fragrant perfume of a pastel green rose-like blossom the size of her head. *This garden is a pretty beautiful place to hang out.*

"Thanks." Sol disappeared through an archway, and a few seconds later Jordan heard the sound of squeaky hinges as some door opened to receive him. The door closed, and she was left alone with the blossoms and the insects that danced among them.

She strolled the terrace at her leisure, sniffing plants and herbs, and trying and failing to place the language root of the identifying glyphs that had been painted onto the tiny signposts thrust into the dirt. They had accents not unlike that of Hebrew, sharp angles of Runes, and the occasional swirling spirals of Sanskrit. But all together, the language was indiscernible to her.

The terrace was enclosed on all sides by a stone wall nearly twice Jordan's height. The exception was a handful of lower narrow ledges scattered about, where a view of Maticaw could be gained. The sounds of distant laughter floating on the humid, sea air drew Jordan to one of these ledges, where she was rewarded with a sprawling view of Maticaw. She hopped up on the thick mantel, flexing her wings for balance and sat cross-legged.

Bright blue water threw off sparkles of the morning sun, already fat and hot. Jordan perched her elbows on her knees and rested her chin in her palm as the wind tugged at her hair. Sailing vessels of all sizes and shapes drifted in and out of the large port. This one tall and slender like a schooner, that one winged and spiked like an Asian spice trader. A small rocky island just beyond the shelter of the bay, with a fortress-like construction on it, turned black as the sun sank low in the sky.

Distant conversations drifted up from the city like puffs of smoke; loud brays of laughter and some harsher sounding exchanges filled the air and made Maticaw feel alive. Peering a little further over the edge, Jordan could see the long drop of a stone wall plummeting for several stories before meeting the winding cobbled streets below. A narrow set of stairs zigzagged up the rocky hillside and wrapped itself around the curved walls of the tower on which Jordan now sat.

Hopping off the ledge, Jordan crossed the terrace and wandered beneath the archway that Sol had passed through. A smaller courtyard opened up with a stone building on one side featuring two huge wooden doors, both closed. A wooden gate at the far end beckoned, and she found the staircase on the other side of it. Jordan looked back at the wooden doors. *There's no sign of Sol yet; surely I have time for just a short, exploratory walk. I'll be back before he even notices I'm missing. Besides, I have wings now and can be back on the terrace in a flash.*

The gate squealed as Jordan pushed through it and descended the curving stone steps. Having the world suddenly wide open on one side, where the edge of the stairs dropped off with no railing or wall, made her heart skip a beat. The wind picked up her hair and whipped it around.

Jordan followed the stairway down to street level and found herself in the midst of a busy city market. Fascinated, she followed the road downward, taking in the small quaint shops and the wares on display. It was like Nishpat, only much bigger and more cosmopolitan. As fascinating as the shops were, they couldn't compare to Maticaw's citizens.

Amongst the humans were countless non-humans, all looking a great deal like someone had taken drawings from a fantasy artist's doodle book and breathed them into life. There had been more than a few moments that hammered home Jordan was surely not on Earth anymore; walking Maticaw's cobbled streets was one of them. A large furry silver rat wearing a vest scampered by on its hind legs. He or she had a burlap sack held in its paws, just like a prim housewife would hold a clutch. A larger creature that still only reached mid-thigh went the other way, rolling a small barrel. His skin was a rich forest green color. The hands that pushed the barrel were three-fingered, and each digit was completed by a single, terrifying claw. One rheumy eye moving independently of the other darted up at her, and she looked away, sure that the creature wouldn't appreciate her staring.

Jordan had just spotted a baby dragon in a basket on a woman's hip and had opened her mouth to ask if she could take a closer look, when the locket at her neck began to drift into the air. Her eyes were trained on the small sapphire blue and yellow creature making creaking noises like a rusty hinge, when a silver blob appeared in her vision somewhere in the vicinity of her chin. Jordan stopped walking and stared at the locket, watching it move. It drifted the way a piece of fluff might catch a current, lazily bobbing in front of her face. She tapped the top of it, and it descended only to float upward again. Baffled, Jordan snatched the locket and stuffed it down her vest, lodging it between her breastbone and the bra that Sohne had given her. She levied her attention back on the dragon.

"Excuse me," Jordan said to the woman with the basket.

Big earrings of a yellow metal that looked like gold swung beside the woman's jaw, and a purple kerchief covered part of her puffy brown hair.

"May I see your dragon?" Jordan asked.

"He is for sale," the woman replied, turning so Jordan could see the scaly baby. "For sale, for sale." She smiled into Jordan's face. "He is very young. Very sweet."

Jordan peered in at the dragon, and he looked up at her, croaking a rusty cry. A little red tongue darted out at her hand as she held her fingers out for him to sniff. Jordan felt her heart begin to melt.

* * *

Sol had been to Cles's laboratory several times already this year and felt that the medicine man might be okay with Sol letting himself into the lab. Sol was on King Konig's business, after all.

"Hello? Cles?" Sol called into the gloom. "Are you here?" The door closed behind him. The dim space smelled of dried herbs, bitters, vinegar, oil, and smoke. Numerous sprawling tabletops were covered in strange looking equipment: distilling devices, small hot plates with multiple wicks underneath, and bottles and jars of all materials, from glass to ceramic to basalt. Copper pipes curled and spiralled gracefully between copper pots and vats. Nearly everything looked very expensive, and in use. In contrast to the mess of the lab and further toward the back wall was a neatly kept library. Well-stocked storage shelves lined and organized with pristine equipment and containers faced the bookshelves.

"Cles?" Sol crossed in front of two yawning furnaces. Both were cold, and black with soot. He peered up the spiral staircase lined with ornate spindles. Sol had never been upstairs, but he figured it was safe to guess that upstairs was Cles's private quarters.

" 'Lo?" Came a raspy cry, followed by a dusky, deep cough. "Whozat?"

"It's Solomon Donda. Is that you, Cles?"

A phlegm-filled laugh answered him. "Course it be me, no one else living here." His voice tightened as though he was working at getting up from laying flat on his back. Perhaps the old Nycht had been napping; he was getting on in years. "You have a deliver?"

"Yes, I have a deliver." Sol smiled. He'd always liked the way Cles phrased things. "You sound unwell." Sol craned his neck, peering up the steps for some sight of the apothecary. "Anything the matter?"

"Nothing, nothing," came the grumbling voice along with the thudding of heavy footsteps. Cles appeared at the top of the steps, propping wire rimmed spectacles on his face, which enlarged his eyes. He began to descend in a laborious, waddling way, his bulk swaying back and forth with every step. " 'Lergic to miniphos plant. Very 'lergic." As if to highlight the proclamation, he followed these words with another explosive coughing attack.

Sol stepped back from the stairs and watched the old Nycht descend. "Sounds like a cold to me," he said, crossing his arms. "And you must be the only Nycht in all of Strixdom who has stairs in his house and takes them daily."

Dusky light from the frosted glass windows illuminated Cles as he descended. The light traveled over the bottoms of his bare feet, over his simple homespun leggings, past his fat leather belt and paunchy belly—which had seen one too many mugs of ale over the years—to his barrel chest and pale lined face. He was chuckling in his usual throaty way, which was made even more hoarse by the phlegm in his chest. "Don't fly much no more." The Nycht ran a hand over his bald head. His grey leathery wings poked up over his head, skinny and flabby, atrophied from lack of use. The hooked claws at the tops of his wings drooped uselessly, the nails cracked and brittle—their climbing days long over.

Sol knew that Cles hadn't flown in several years. A body that big would be hell to carry, even for a strong Nycht. Regular use was critical for any Strix who wanted to keep the ability to fly as they aged. The part of the population who didn't care enough for flying to do it every day had baffled Sol since he'd been a young Arpak. Flying was Sol's life and independence, his freedom and happiness.

"Between we," Cles said, winking conspiratorially, "I'm considering to cut."

Sol blinked at the casual way Cles delivered that he was thinking about making this irreversible operation. Losing one's wings by passing out of Oriceran meant they could grow back when fed enough magic. Losing one's wings by amputation meant the wings would be gone forever. Sol was sure the Elves could probably reverse amputation if they were paid enough, but anyone who amputated did it because they were certain they no longer wanted wings. In some cases, the Rodanian Council might hand down a sentence of amputation to a criminal, but it was extremely rare, reserved as punishment for murder or acts of treason that could lead to regicide. Sol swallowed hard at the idea of any Strix having their wings amputated, on purpose or by the Rodanian justice system.

"At this point for my little life," Cles rasped. "They are more nuisance than blessing. But enough of this old Nycht. You have a deliver?"

Sol handed the yellow envelope to Cles with the words, "It's from Juer."

"Course it from him." Cles took the envelope in one meaty fist and bumped his other one against his chest as he gave another rasping cough. "It always from doctor." Cles turned away and lumbered to where the light was better. "Always a doctor. Always a Juer," he muttered. The lab fell silent while he read. After a little while he gave a harrumph. "He want what I only have so small of."

Cles swayed heavily over to the cabinetry along the side wall, and opened the doors to reveal shelves full of various containers, each marked by a hand printed label. He rooted through the supply, gently tapping the tops of various jars with the pads of his blunt fingers. He selected a small jar of black liquid and leaned over a small desk under the window.

"Wait," Cles said to Sol, hand patting at the air, gesturing that Sol should sit. "I write slow. Rest please, or you make me anxiety. Needs quiet for thoughts. When you be tranquil, Cles be tranquil."

His better nature thus appealed to, Sol perched on a nearby

stool. The tips of Sol's wings shifted to cross at his ankles, hovering just out of the dust.

Cles sat as well, but the old Nycht's approach was to kick his wingtips with a heel to move them out from under the stool's three legs. He reached for a piece of paper and a pencil and scratched out a short note. "I not have what he ask." Cles grumbled. "Lapita; must be sick, or crops gone bad. I know not."

Sol felt a niggling rodent of anxiety burrow into his gut. This probably wasn't good. Until now, Cles always had whatever Juer asked for, and plenty of it besides. Cles had always made a point of saying so and encouraged Sol to purchase extra of whatever concoction the doctor had ordered. Sol was a courier; his job was to deliver important messages on behalf of the king and the king's staff. But it was sometimes impossible not to get sucked into palace drama as he came into direct contact with the parties on either end of a delivery. He wondered which important Arpak the medicine was for.

"How much is he asking for?" Sol asked, getting to his feet.

"Too much. Don't have raw material." Cles folded up the note and stood.

Sol frowned. *Obviously.*

"He ask for lapita many times, and many times I give." The big shoulders rose and fell. "Lapita in short supply now." He held out the letter and the small jar to Sol. "This all I have. Last of stock. Take it. If it for Juer, it much important."

"What if it's not enough?" Sol took the small jar sloshing with black liquid and the letter and tucked both into his satchel.

Cles waved a plate-sized hand. "Find new source, or wait til source replenish. I see many things go in, go out." He rubbed his stubbly chin with his fingers. "Lapita no different. Is eighteen coin." He held open his palm.

"Eighteen!" This price was outrageous for any concoction, even lapita.

"Is commodity, so-" Cles shrugged. "Supply go down, price go up. Is simple economy."

Sol frowned and dug into his satchel. He'd picked up lapita many times before, and it had never been so pricey. It wasn't his money—it was the king's money. Still, he had to report the outrageous price to the royal accountants, and they wouldn't be happy that the price of lapita had tripled. Sol counted out the price and spilled the gold into Cles's hands.

"Pleasure being business," Cles said as he pocketed the coin.

"Doing business," corrected Sol, still perturbed at being charged so much. "The auxiliary verbs in English—"

Cles's eyes glazed over and his jaw sagged a bit.

"Nevermind. I'll show myself out." Sol left the dim, odd-smelling lab and stepped out into the gardens and sunlight. "Ready to…"

But Jordan was not on the terrace.

CHAPTER 3

It didn't take Sol long to spot Jordan from the sky over Maticaw. Her blonde hair and bright yellow feathers caught his eye like a beacon on a stormy night. She seemed to be in active conversation with a gypsy woman dressed almost entirely in purple. Sol's Arpak vision sharpened on the pair. There was a basket on the gypsy woman's hip, but whatever was in the basket was blocked by the golden arch of Jordan's wing. He banked and drifted, finding an open space in the street to land in.

Dodging merchants and shoppers, Sol wound his way to Jordan. The gypsy had a cloud of brown curls puffing up from a purple headscarf, and bangles twanged from her wrists. A holey, knitted shawl was tied around her waist and trailed in the dust of the street. Her face was lined with age, but her brown eyes were keen with intelligence, the whites very white and brown very rich. Her expression was an interesting blend of kindness and craftiness.

"Jordan, I'm finished. Ready to go?" Sol said at Jordan's elbow. "I have a delivery for Upper Rodania." His irritation that she'd not been on the terrace waiting for him was only mild, as she'd been so easy to find. "Wish you hadn't left the—whoa!" His eyes dropped to the small blue dragon perched in Jordan's palm. "I don't know if you've noticed, but there's a dragon on you."

The little reptile was no larger than a rat and had diamond-shaped scales of bright blue. A yellow patch, nearly identical to the brightest yellow of Jordan's own wings, ran from its throat to its chest and along the insides of each leg. Its dark blue wings were folded against its back, and its long tail was wrapped around Jordan's arm like a spiral bracelet. Small, blunted nails the color of midnight sprang from short little claws, which were clutched around Jordan's wrist and in between her fingers. The dragon had shiny black orbs for eyes that were too big for its face, which gave it a mousy quality. Two little holes on either sides of its head served as ears, and two slender blue horns curved gracefully back from its skull. The scales that ran over its brow and neck were brighter and smoother than the rest - almost pearly. This dragon was well fed and well taken care of.

The reptile cocked his head at the sounds of the women's voices, his tongue darting out now and then, smelling the air or maybe the situation. Sol had studied dragons during his training, but more about how to recognize and avoid the dangerous ones than anything else. This little reptile, covered in his jewel-like scales and observing the world with a bright intelligent gaze, didn't look like any of the ones Sol had studied. It also looked like a baby.

Jordan blinked up at Sol, bewildered. "I'm sorry you had to come find me. I meant to be back at the terrace before you were finished. Yes, I'm ready to go, but we seem to have a problem." To illustrate, she held the dragon out to the gypsy woman.

The gypsy reached out for the dragon, and the dragon squawked and skittered up Jordan's arm to perch on her shoulder. Jordan winced at the sharp claws running the terrain of her body.

The gypsy dropped the basket at her feet and put her hands on her hips with a huff. "He has imprinted on you, girl. You have to buy him. There is nothing else to be done." The gypsy looked up at Sol, as though hoping to find an ally in him. "Tell her."

"That's just a sales tactic," said Sol, reaching for the dragon. "Nothing more." He scooped the reptile up and handed it back to the gypsy, who glowered at him.

"It's not a trick," she grumped. "Berla is many things, but she's not a trickster." She took the dragon back and picked up the basket, setting him inside it and perching it on her hip. She looked down expectantly. "You watch. It's not a trick."

"Let's go." Sol put a hand on Jordan's shoulder, and they began to head back toward the stairs leading up to the apothecary's terrace, where they could catch an updraft.

There was a throaty, despairing scream behind them. As they turned, a flapping blue blur fell into the dust at Jordan's feet. The little dragon turned his liquid black eyes up to Jordan and gave a plaintive cry.

"Oh, look at him." Jordan's expression melted and she squatted. She picked up the dusty creature and brushed him off. The dragon leaned into her touch and emitted a clicking rumble from deep in his chest, a reptilian purr. Jordan stood, cupping the creature next to her stomach. "He likes me."

Sol rubbed a hand down his face and sighed.

"He more than likes you," said the gypsy woman, approaching with the basket dangling from one hand. "Dragon imprinting is a bond for life. It's not a joke. If you don't take him with you, he'll die of a broken heart."

Jordan gasped and looked up at Sol, eyes beginning to take on a pleading glaze.

"Jordan, dragons aren't allowed on Rodania," he said, firmly but with compassion. "I'm sorry. They grow to be enormous and, not least of all, dangerous. Let's go, we're wasting time—"

"This one won't," interjected the gypsy woman. "He's a Predoian Miniature. He won't get any bigger than what he is now."

Sol looked down at the tiny reptile now nuzzling between Jordan's elbow and ribs. "Really? He looks like a baby to me. He can't even fly yet."

"He is young but he is full-grown." The woman lifted her chin. "I know dragons. And don't insult me by saying it is some kind of ruse. I care for my dragons; they are not just my business. I do not send them to where they will be unhappy."

Jordan stroked under the dragon's chin. His mouth opened and his tongue snaked out as he dropped his jaw into her hand. "Who knew reptiles could be so affectionate? Are miniature ones allowed on Rodania?"

Sol hesitated.

Jordan's face brightened. "They are?"

"Yes, but he can't fly, and neither of us is equipped to take on a pet right now." Sol scooped the dragon up a second time and handed him to the woman in purple. "Hold him, please. Don't let him follow her. We're leaving now."

The gypsy took the dragon reflexively but her eyes widened in fear. "I can't do that! Do you want me to lose a finger or an eye?"

Sol snatched the rope lying in the bottom of the basket. "Then tie him up and wait until we're out of sight." His nimble fingers fashioned a noose and he slipped it over the dragon's head, scooped him up, and bent at the nearest tree. He tied the dragon to the tree trunk and stood up, satisfied. "There, now he can't hurt you."

The gypsy woman rolled her eyes. "You are not even an amateur."

Sol steered Jordan toward the steps. "Let's. Go." There was another screech as the two Arpaks strode away. "Ignore him, Jordan."

"But—" Jordan looked back over her shoulder. "What if she's right? What if he dies?"

They couldn't ignore the second, much louder screech, which was followed by a panicked flapping of wings and desperate snapping of jaws. The dragon strained at the cord. He turned his head almost completely backward and sawed through the rope with his back teeth like it was nothing but floss. He came at Jordan in a flapping run and took a bounce at her feet. The reptile landed awkwardly on Jordan's shoulder, his wings flexed for balance. He looped his head under her chin with a distressed whistle.

The gypsy followed, her hands on her hips. "Many would sell everything they own in order to have a dragon imprint with them. You are stupid if you do not see the benefit of this."

Sol rolled his eyes. Jordan wrapped her fingers gently around the dragon and held him next to her heart, murmuring soft words.

"You do not need to take care of a dragon. They take care of you." She jabbed a long-nailed finger into Sol's face. "You do not need to feed them. They are our most deadly predator. You do not need to clean up after them. They do their business in the woods because it's the only time they feel vulnerable," she cocked her head with a faint smile, "and a little embarrassed." She looked down at the dragon with affection. "And they will love you until they die." She looked back at Sol and Jordan, and her face hardened. "You are a fool if you do not take him with you. And you would also be murderers."

"Easy now," muttered Sol, flushing faintly under Jordan's gaze. He was rapidly losing this fight and soon he would be the bad guy, if he wasn't already. "We didn't come here for a dragon. How much is he?"

The woman lost a little of her composure. "Sixty coin," she said, shuffling from one foot to the other, purple skirt swaying.

Sol barked an outraged laugh. "We don't even want him!"

"I do," said Jordan shyly.

Sol stared at her.

Jordan's bashfulness turned to certainty. "I want him. I'll find a way to pay you back for him. Please."

"How?" Sol put his hands on his hips. "With what gold?"

Jordan shrugged. "I'll find a way. Money is easy to get, you just have to be creative."

Sol groaned inwardly. "I'll give you five coin for him." He said to the gypsy woman. "If you care so much for him, you'll agree to it. We did not come here for a dragon; he was thrust upon us. If you don't accept my offer, the dragon stays, and you'll be as much a party to murder as we would be." Sol shrugged and crossed his arms to communicate he was finished negotiating.

The gypsy woman's mouth dropped open but quickly snapped shut, realizing how he'd trapped her. Her brown eyes flashed from one solemn face to the other, then to the little dragon now perched peacefully on Jordan's shoulder. "Make it ten coin, and let's say no more about it."

Mutely, Sol dug the coins from his satchel and dropped them into her upturned palm with a frown. "Good day."

"Wait," the gypsy woman said, opening the bag at her hip and rifling through it. She retrieved a small folded piece of paper. "Here are his papers. You might need them."

Sol took the paper and opened it, reading the handwritten certificate saying that the dragon was a Predoian Miniature born in Maticaw the year before. Sol glanced from the page to the gypsy and was about to ask if it was even legitimate—after all, the dragon couldn't even fly properly yet—but he thought better of it. They didn't have time for this. He tucked the page into his satchel and nodded goodbye to the dragon peddler. The Arpaks left the gypsy woman standing in the street, with a moue of unhappiness on her face.

"You'll have to carry him," Sol warned as they made their way up to Cles's terrace. "Are you okay with that? I can do it, if you like." Even though she didn't complain about it, Sol knew Jordan was still sore from the journey from Charra-Rae. It was a long way to go for an Arpak who'd just gotten her wings.

"I can do it," said Jordan with a smile. She followed at his heels as they climbed the steps. "How was your delivery, by the way?"

"Not good," Sol grunted. "Cles didn't have what he was asked for. I don't think Juer will be happy."

"Who is Juer?" Jordan had begun to pant and blew out a big exhale as they reached the terrace, flexing her wings in preparation. She and Sol crossed the landing to the balcony.

"The royal physician," said Sol. He hopped up onto the platform built into the terrace railing and held a hand out to Jordan. "Are you ready?" His wings opened out halfway.

Jordan stepped up and looked down at the city below them, her tummy quivering. "This part still freaks me out a bit." Her wings opened out, the feathers brushing the tops of the foliage reaching up from the garden patches.

"Want me to take him?" Sol nodded at the little blue reptile cupped now in Jordan's hands.

"No, I've got him." Her eyes were bright and her face pink. "How far to Rodania, did you say?"

"Five to six hours, depending on the wind. We have to bank north and follow the coast for a bit. Storms gather between Maticaw and Rodania, but they're easily avoided by going north."

Jordan faced the sea and stepped to the edge of the stone ledge, built just so Strix could drop off and catch an updraft. Maticaw stretched out before her, its rooftop terraces and towers cascading down the steep mountainsides to the sea. Her heart vaulted into her throat, as it seemed to do without fail whenever she had to take off. She looked down at the little dragon, contemplating that she now had a companion for life, if the gypsy was to be believed. Jordan felt the ties between her and Oriceran tighten.

Miserably, Jordan thought of her father and wished he could

be with her to experience all of this. *Did he receive my message? Did it frighten him? What am I thinking, of course it did.*

"Jordan? You okay?"

Jordan turned to Sol, eyes glistening. She brushed at her face. "What should we call him?" She looked down at the reptile to hide her emotion. She was still so relieved that Sol hadn't left her to fend for herself in this strange land that the idea of burdening him further with her problems was abhorrent to her.

"Uh," Sol gazed at the tiny creature's sapphire blue scales. He was actually a spectacular specimen; a real beauty, for a reptile. Not that Sol had seen many dragons in his lifetime, but the ones he had seen were a dull gray color, and somewhat misshapen. "Blue?"

" 'Blue'!" Jordan laughed. The dragon looked up at the sound of her laughter and rattled off a purr in his throat. "No points for creativity. Don't worry," she looked down into the dragon's face, "we won't call you Blue," she crooned.

"Jordan—"

"Yes, I'm ready." She clutched the dragon against her chest with both hands so he'd feel secure. "Don't worry. I won't drop you," she murmured. With a squeal and a gasp, she spread her wings and hopped from the platform. She dipped face-first toward Maticaw and banked upward at the last moment, just missing a weathervane spire, which spun as she passed.

CHAPTER 4

The Kacy Estate

THERE HAS to be a logical explanation for this.

Allan paced back and forth in front of the 'booze bureau'—that's what Jordan called it—pausing at either end to eye the strange glass bugs in his bourbon bottle. Since he was now out of bourbon, the glass in his hand carried single-malt scotch instead. The normally smooth oaky flavor had turned to diesel on his tongue. Still, he was on his second tumbler, and his hundredth journey across the carpeted floor.

These same bugs might enable me to contact Jordy, but how? The bugs had gone dormant and rested in the bottom of the bottle, along with traces of bourbon still left inside. As though to reassure himself that he'd not imagined the whole thing, Allan tapped a finger against the glass. Two of the bugs sprouted legs and crawled over their companions to the glass walls of the bottle, where they began to climb, ever optimistic that the cork had been removed since the last time they'd checked. How glass could cling to glass was beyond Allan, but the bugs were somehow able to scale the slippery surface, their tiny feet click click clicking.

Allan set his drink on the bureau, rooted his cell out of his pocket, and scrolled through his contacts until he found Inspector Cranston's number. His thumb hovered over the green 'Call' icon. He had to have answers, and if Cranston could talk all kinds of crap about avian-human chimeras, he'd have to be open to the idea of parallel universe bugs spelling out messages from his missing daughter.

"I *am* crazy," he whispered, but he hit the dial button anyway. He lifted the cell to his ear, failing to block out the *tink tink* of bug legs. He turned his back to the bourbon bottle and wandered to the archway between the parlor and the foyer. Bracing against the doorjamb, Allan sank to the floor and listened to the ringtone. The phone rang twice, and then clicked as it was answered.

"Senator Kacy?" Cranston's voice came through clear and crisp. "What can I do for you?"

"Cranston." Allan's heart doubled its speed, and his palms suddenly felt cold and clammy. He felt his resolve weaken. "I – have there been any developments in the case? Have you found anything else out about the – uh, the chimera?"

"Nothing new, sir," Cranston replied, then cleared his throat. "I hesitated to tell you about the blood for this very reason. I didn't want you to worry. I assure you that everything is under control, sir. We'll find Jordan and we'll bring her back. I promise."

Allan cringed. He hated when people said 'I promise'. Cranston was just a man, and when men made promises, they nearly always broke them. Allan thought that it was one of the many ways God kept people humble, as if to say, *'I can make promises. But you shouldn't.'*

Allan's eyes tracked to the bourbon bottle where two of the bugs were jammed into the neck. As he watched, they both put their legs away and fell with a *clink* into the pile of their companions below.

His mouth formed a grim line. Jordan's bug message had told him the answer—she'd fallen through a portal. *How is it possible? How can any of this be real? Maybe they slipped drugs into my bourbon and I've hallucinated the whole event. That doesn't explain the bugs, though.* He'd felt them beneath his fingertips; they were all he could see now.

Glass marbles moving and–

Cranston was talking. Allan had almost forgotten he was still holding the phone to his ear.

"…get some rest, Senator Kacy. You'll feel better after a good night's sleep."

"Wait, Cranston." He took a steadying breath. "I've found something."

The *tuk tuk* of a helicopter's blades overhead sliced through his certainty like a hot blade through butter. He was a senator; he was under watch, under protection, and he sure as hell couldn't afford to look crazy at a time like this. At any time, really. Even a whiff of crazy equated to weakness, loss of all credibility, loss of any pull he might have.

Loss of power and credibility could endanger his life, and Jordan's.

"What did you find?" Cranston asked.

Allan gritted his teeth at the bugs.

"What did you find, Senator?"

"It's, uh, it's a picture of Jordan. I thought you might need an up-to-date one for your records."

"Oh," Cranston replied, and the disappointment leaked through the phone. "That's fine, sir. I'll come over in the morning to collect the photographs."

"Goodnight." Allan hung up before he blurted out anything about glowing marble bugs and portals. He let out a long exhale. "What do I do?" He forced himself upright and readjusted his glasses.

The bugs were unconcerned by his plight; their fat glassy

bodies lay dormant again in the bottom of the bottle, looking like so many eggs.

"What am I supposed to *do*?" Allan asked again, frustration mounting. He lifted the bottle and poked at the glass with his fingertip. "You in there. Things. What am I supposed to do?" He'd neatly crossed the line from tipsy into drunk quite some time ago.

If Jordan used these little suckers to send me a message, perhaps I can use them to send one back. I can ask her where she is, how to get there, and whether she needs anything.

What if she's hurt? Or cold? Or lost? Fear pasted his tongue to the roof of his mouth.

Decades had passed since Jaclyn's disappearance, but he'd harbored a secret fear ever since it'd happened. He'd tended to it in the silence of sleepless nights, and nurtured the fear like one would care for an orchid—this belief that someone would one day take his baby away from him. That he'd lose his daughter, the only person who mattered anymore. It was unthinkable, which of course meant that he thought about it far too frequently.

And now, it had come to pass.

These little glass balls were the only tie he had left to her. "I'll be damned if I let this happen," Allan whispered. "I'll be damned if I just wait around and do nothing!"

He clutched the bottle in his fist and charged through the house, out the back door, down the deck stairs, and toward that five-hundred-year-old oak tree and its swinging chair. He was buoyed up on scotch and belief.

I'll contact Jordan again. It has *to be real.*

Allan dropped to his knees in front of the old oak and said a quick silent prayer. *Let me see her again. Let me bring her back. Let me talk to her. Please, she's all I have left. She's my little girl.*

An image rose from the dust of his memories–Jordan as a five-year-old, her chubby hands squished against his cheeks.

'You're the best daddy borned. Smartess, too.'

'Smartest, sweetheart.'

'That's you.'

Tears squeezed out of the corners of his eyes, and he lifted the bottle. His breath caught in his chest. The bugs were glowing. Those two yellow eyes on each glassy marble had reappeared. His heart skipped to a strange rhythm to see how they'd responded to being near the tree. More proof that there was some invisible portal here.

"I need your help," Allan said to the bugs. "I need to speak to Jordan. I'm going to let you out, but you have to help me, okay?"

They seemed to stare at him, unmoving now. *Is that a sign that they agree?*

He uncorked the bottle with a ceremonious hollow pop, and then laid the bottle in the grass on its side.

The bugs crawled out one by one, and scurried toward the tree.

"No, wait! No, you have to do the message," Allan said, and grabbed one, then another. He tried arranging them, but their glassy bodies darted toward the tree as soon as he released them. He tried to gather them up all at once between his palms, as many as he could, but each time he placed them in a pattern, they scuttled off again, always toward the oak tree.

"Stop it," he commanded. "I have to send a message to Jordan!"

The bugs didn't stop. They glowed brighter, their yellow eyes blending into one, blindingly bright light. They became like small stars. They reached the tree, crawled up its roots, and swarmed over the bark. They blazed now, so bright that Allan had to blink against the glare.

Allan stifled panic and tears and raised his arm to block the light. "Please," he said. "Jordy."

The light evaporated and was replaced by darkness and silence. Nothing moved; not even a whisper of wind in the long grass, or the creak of the swinging chair. He lowered his arm. The bugs were gone, and it was too quiet.

"Hello?" he croaked, staring at the tree where something was *happening*.

The center of the tree moved and blurred. A hole widened in the fabric of Allan's reality; the bark of the tree melted away and pulled back, stretching open like it was made of latex. The hole wobbled and expanded, exposing a strange deep blackness which changed color from dark to midnight blue, then to the bright glaring blue of a clear summer sky. The radiant azure rim stretched outward, undulating and widening with a serpentine sway.

The hole broadened, and the blue haze at its center dissipated and revealed... something else. Another place, another time, a view of–

"It *is* a portal," he whispered, and broke out in a cold sweat. The bugs hadn't sent a message to her, but they had left a hole, a path, a doorway.

It didn't matter if the bugs had heard him and done it on purpose or if it was purely an accident, a result of their travel back home. They'd created an opportunity. Allan scrambled upright and swayed on the spot. The edges of the hole in the fabric of Earth's universe tightened, and Allan gasped—the opportunity, it seemed, would be very short. 'Now or never' took on new meaning. He glanced back only once at his plantation home, his jaw tightening with resolve. He could no more say no to this opportunity than he could prevent the grass from growing up around the old house.

He clenched his fists, faced the new world, and entered it to find his daughter.

CHAPTER 5

"We have to descend here," Sol shouted over the wind buffeting their eardrums.

Jordan nodded and clutched the dragon closer to her chest as they banked and dropped out of the stream of cool air that had been keeping them aloft for the last hour. The five-hour journey had not been as difficult as the one from Charra-Rae to Maticaw, and Jordan was beginning to understand how air currents behaved differently over water than they did over land. It was almost as though the sea air was made to buoy up wings and carry them for miles and miles, almost effortlessly. The currents over land were shorter, choppier, and changed temperature and direction quickly. Maybe it had something to do with altitude; Jordan didn't know, but she was grateful for the difference of having water beneath her.

Passing over an endless sea and allowing her wings to do most of the work meant that Jordan could phase into a meditative place. The endless stretch of blue on blue, sky over sea, and the soft haze where the two met, made her feel partially deprived of sensation.

The currents whispered under their wings, caressing and lifting. Jordan had to remind herself to close her nictitating membranes to protect her eyes from wind and ultraviolet light. One of these days she supposed she would do it without thinking, just as she was learning to fly without thinking. Sol had been right. It was like walking—you didn't have to tell your legs to move, they just did.

Below them was a speck in the sea, a small disc-shaped platform with a transparent dome protecting it. Two Nychts could be seen moving about under the dome. A deck extended around the glass dome, and it was on this that the two Arpaks finally landed and closed up their wings.

Jordan took a deep breath and stretched her shoulders and back, letting the dragon climb up to rest in the cradle made between her wings and the back of her neck.

"How much further to Rodania?" she asked, her eyes glazing over as she looked out at the empty horizon, stretching out in all directions. They'd already been flying for hours; the sun was well past its crest, and there was still no land visible anywhere. Her stomach dropped. She was tired. *How did Sol misjudge the distance so badly? Doesn't he make the journey between Maticaw and Rodania all the time?*

"We're here," replied Sol. He signalled to the Nychts inside the dome, and one of them nodded at Sol and held up two fingers, letting them know he'd be out to address them momentarily.

"We are?" Jordan scanned the endless horizon around them. "What do you mean? I thought Rodania was a huge city?"

"It is." Sol smiled at Jordan's confusion. "I can see it, but you can't. You'll be able to as soon as we register you."

"Oh." She assumed this was like having to present your passport at customs. "I don't have any documentation," said Jordan. "Will that be a problem?"

Sol shook his head. "They can see you're Arpak. That's the first and most important box ticked. Believe me, it's a lot more difficult to get in the first time if you're not Strix."

A square seam outlining a door appeared in the glass dome, then popped out and lifted, rolling up the curved walls of the dome on invisible hinges like some space-age garage door. One of the Nychts stepped outside. He was short and wiry with a dark tan and hair so blonde it was nearly white. He reminded Jordan of a surfer with tough-looking skin and wiry arms. A pair of dark glasses perched on the top of his head. The Nycht might have been beautiful, in a weathered sort of way, but for the dark purple bruising which cupped each eye. The whites of his eyes were threaded with capillaries. He looked as though he hadn't had a good night's sleep in his life.

"Sol. Welcome home," he said with a sleepy nod. His eyes drifted to Jordan, blinking slowly.

"Thanks, Pabs," said Sol. "How's the new position?"

"The shiftwork is killing me, but you can't complain about the view. Hello, miss," he addressed Jordan. "Welcome to Rodania." He took her hand.

"Thanks." Jordan looked down at where he turned her hand over to expose her palm.

Pabs produced a small silver device.

Jordan looked to Sol and he nodded reassuringly. Bringing the device to the pad of her thumb, Pabs murmured, "A little prick."

Jordan jumped as a small needle stabbed her finger and vacuumed her blood into a tiny reservoir in the same moment.

"Sorry, it only hurts for a second," Pabs said. Then he spotted the dragon curled up like a puppy in the tripod of Jordan's neck and wings.

Pabs put his glasses on his nose, obscuring his eyes completely behind dark glass. "Hello, little fellow," he addressed the reptile. Then he removed his glasses and peered at Sol. "Dragons aren't allowed in Rodania. You know this."

"Miniatures are," Sol said. "Check the bylaws. We'll wait. You can process her blood in the meantime."

Pabs looked doubtful but set his glasses on his head and stepped through the doorway into the dome. He moved to a small machine of blinking lights and switches. He flicked a switch, and a tiny tray slid out, into which he deposited the vial of Jordan's blood. The tray slid inward. The Nycht bent and blew over a sensor, and the machine chimed loud enough that Jordan and Sol could hear it from the deck. Then Pabs went to a wall filled with scrolls on one side and what looked like tiny vials of smoke on the other, all resting on their own little pegs. Pabs stood in front of the strange looking wall and scratched his head. He called something over to the other Nycht, who sat bent over a desk. His redheaded colleague looked up from his work and blinked at Pabs, nose wrinkling in thought. He looked almost as tired as Pabs did. He got up and stood in front of the wall, shoulder to shoulder beside Pabs, and the two of them blinked up at the wall.

"Why do they look like they've been in a barfight?" Jordan whispered to Sol while they watched this dazed and bemused play unfold before them.

"They're new. Pabs used to work in one of the mines in Lower Rodania," explained Sol. "And Innes used to apprentice with a millwright. They took the border-guard position a few weeks ago, but haven't adjusted to the daylight hours yet. It always takes a while."

"Oh, because Nychts are nocturnal," Jordan added as it clicked into place. "Toth told me."

Sol frowned at the mention of Toth. "Do you have the certificate the gypsy gave you?"

"You put it in your satchel," replied Jordan. "Remember?"

Sol put a hand to his leather bag. "Right." He retrieved the crumpled registration certificate. "I doubt this is legit, but it's all we've got."

"Will it be a problem?" Jordan put a hand up to her neck and the dragon lifted his head, got to his feet, and tottered onto her palm. She cradled him in front of her stomach.

"Don't think so. But I have never tried to bring a dragon into Rodania before." He lowered his voice. "To be honest, because I work for the government, I almost never have trouble with these things. Even when maybe I should."

"Lucky you," Jordan said with raised brows. "Special treatment."

Pabs emerged from the dome with another device in his hand. "Looks like you're right. Miniatures are allowed, provided they are purebloods. "Uh," he plopped his glasses back onto his face, covering what looked like an expression of trepidation. "May I?" He held out his hand for the dragon.

Jordan lifted the reptile and looked him in the eye. "It only hurts for a second," she said into the shining black eyes, having no idea if he understood any of her words. Even if he didn't, maybe the meaning was clear. The dragon blinked.

"Says to take it from a haunch," said Pabs. "Right here." He reached a fingertip out and pointed at the fleshy part of the dragon's hind-leg. He raised the device and hesitated. The reptile whipped his head around to watch the device approaching, his jaws opened and his tongue flicked out at the device.

"Just do it, man," said Sol. "Dragons can smell fear."

"That's not comforting," murmured Pabs.

"It's alright," said Jordan. She touched the dragon under his chin.

Quickly Pabs touched the needle to the haunch, and the blood was extracted. The dragon rattled out a hiss and flicked his tongue at Pabs. He skittered up Jordan's arm to his safe place above her wings, shaking his hind leg like a dog that'd just peed.

"That wasn't so bad." Pabs blew out a breath. "His papers?"

Sol handed Pabs the registration.

"Name?"

Sol blinked at Jordan with a lopsided grin, waiting.

Jordan shot Sol a murderous look. "You knew he was going to ask for a name, didn't you?"

Sol shrugged.

Jordan let out a sigh. "Blue. I guess."

Pabs nodded. "Last name?"

"Uh…Kacy."

"I'll be right back." Pabs went back into the dome of his office. He repeated the same routine with the dragon's blood, only sliding it into a compartment on the other side of the machine.

"You twit," Jordan glared at Sol. "Now I *have* to call him 'Blue'."

"You can change it if you really want to. It'll just cost about fifty coin." Sol gave her a wolfish grin. "Besides, it does suit him. You have to admit that."

She thwacked him on the shoulder. "A dragon deserves an awesome name. Something cool and noble and multi-syllabic."

"Like what?"

"I don't know. Like 'Archimedes' or something."

"Archi-" Sol guffawed. "He's the size of a rodent! Why would you ever saddle him with a ponderous name like 'Archimedes'?"

Blue gave a small startled sneeze, and Jordan winced and wiped the back of her neck.

"See, he hates it."

"I think he resents that you've compared him to a rodent, actually."

Just then the world went black for Jordan, and the pressure in her ears grew. She gasped and reached out a flailing hand. "Sol!"

"It's alright," he said, taking her hand. "It'll be over in a moment."

Her heart rate tripled, and her free hand flew to her face. "Why can't I see? What's wrong with my ears?" She flexed her jaw in an effort to pop them.

"It's better if you relax."

"What is with you Oricerans not warning people before you—Whoa!" Her vision returned, and the pressure in her ears released followed by a long dwindling whine as though a steamboat was sailing away into the great beyond and let off a blast of its whistle. What remained was a faint high-pitched ringing in Jordan's ears, as though she'd been standing next to a pounding speaker at a heavy metal concert the night before.

"Sol!" Jordan put both hands to her cheeks and gaped at the world that had appeared where, a moment before, there had only been blank horizon stretching out into eternity.

Three titanic islands stacked one above the other like an off-kilter cake loomed in the distance.

"Welcome to Lower, Middle and Upper Rodania," said Sol at her shoulder.

Lower Rodania was an island on the water, vast and mountainous; it was difficult to see where it ended. Only a short dash of ocean horizon on either side gave away its island nature. A foul yellow cloud hovered over the south side of the island, reminding Jordan of the haze over big cities back home.

"What's the pollution from? Surely you don't have vehicles and factories?"

"Sure we do!" Sol exclaimed. "Lower Rodania is the seat of industry and a very productive place. On days where the wind is still, dust and exhaust from the mines hangs there until the wind picks up again, and moves it along."

"Huh." Jordan's eyes tracked upward, to the archipelago hovering over Lower Rodania.

Middle Rodania was smaller than Lower Rodania and hovered far above and off-kilter to the landmass below it. Puffs of white cloud shrouded the bases of tower spires and jutting rock. A mountain range rose up in the center of Middle Rodania, and a ring of architecture encrusted it like a crown of jewels. Sunlight glinted off granite, marble, and what looked almost like pearl walls. Middle Rodania threw a long oval shadow over part of Lower Rodania and the sea beyond.

"Is it…" Jordan squinted at the floating mass, "…moving?"

"Yes. Middle Rodania makes a long slow orbit around Lower. If you stand on Middle's edge and look down, you can see how the shore of Middle and Lower line up," Sol explained, gesturing at the sky to illustrate. "Like one huge cog rotating around another."

"Why?" Jordan breathed the question, for she was so awed she could hardly find words. *How is this miracle accomplished?*

"It keeps the shadow off any one area of Lower Rodania for too long. Lower Rodania is also agricultural and needs a lot of sunlight. Most of our food is grown there."

Jordan raised her eyes to Upper Rodania. So high up, it looked about the size of a cookie; all she could make out was the underside. Long jagged stalactites of earth poked downward through a pillow of fluffy cloud. The rest was invisible above the cumulus.

"Does Upper Rodania move as well?"

Sol shook his head. "It doesn't need to."

"Is it cold way up there?"

"On the contrary, it's quite temperate." Sol gave a satisfied smile and crossed his arms. He was proud of his home city; Rodania was a marvel of nature and magical engineering. There was no other place like it on Oriceran, as far as he knew.

Jordan's eyes scanned the skies and the slowly rotating islands. "What keeps them moving?"

"Magic, of course."

"But you said Strix don't have magic."

"Not so much; although there are some among our number who have the gene for a few enchantments. We have many other talents and products, which we trade in exchange for Elf magic to keep our city aloft and in orbit."

Jordan's eyes widened. "Isn't that dangerous? What if the Elves decide they don't want to trade with you anymore?"

Sol laughed. "That could never happen. Not in our lifetimes, anyway. We have a five-thousand-year contract with them, an incorruptible deal."

"What happens at the end of five thousand years?"

Sol shrugged. "The same as with any other contract. We renegotiate based on the current economic value of our republic. It's part of what keeps our society progressive. We are always working to increase our worth. Our council members," he paused. "Whatever else they may be, are excellent business people. Rodania is extremely wealthy."

"But what if you can't renegotiate and have to break with the Elves?"

"In that case, the Elves would lower Middle and Upper Rodania into the sea, and we would become a nation of islands," he spread his hands wide, "instead of the famed floating city."

"Oh." This satisfied Jordan's questions about the elvish contract for the time being. "How come I couldn't see it before?"

"That is also part of our border magic. You weren't registered, so it was invisible to you. You've given your blood, from now on, you'll always be able to see Rodania."

"I only have to give blood the one time?"

"That's right. The magic will remember you, now."

Just then, Blue gave a hollow whistle and shook his head as though to relieve himself of some fly, buzzing in his ear holes. Jordan stroked his head and he calmed at her touch. "I guess that means Blue can always enter Rodania too, now."

"Yes. He might even be the only dragon currently allowed in our city." Sol looked down at the little reptile, "It can happen, but generally Arpaks aren't known for taking pets." Sol crooked a smile at the odd pair.

"You hear that, Blue?" Jordan murmured as Blue pressed his cool scales into her palm. "You're a very special dragon." She looked up, craning her neck to gaze at the furthest floating island. "If Middle Rodania is that beautiful, what does Upper Rodania look like?"

"You're about to find out," Sol said with a grin, spreading his wings. "That's where I live."

CHAPTER 6

A torrent of sound encased Allan and dragged him forward into blackness. A thousand urgent whispers filled his ears and clawed at his thoughts. Then a white-hot light blazed into view, and the whispers stopped. His crunched eyelids peeled back, yet he saw nothing. Nothing at all except whiteness and, slowly, a tinge of blue. The sensation of falling made him feel suddenly sick, his stomach clawing up his throat. Heat blasted him, and Allan slammed chest-first into a hot pile of dust. The breath knocked from his lungs as a cloud of fine particles puffed up around him. He sucked in a breath and promptly choked as his mouth filled with powder. He spat and squeezed his eyes closed, then opened them again. Sweat bled out onto his forehead, beads of moisture ran down his spine and gathered behind his knees.

Where am I? Jordan? His mind whirled, spinning like a top, slowly losing balance and momentum. Had he spoken the words or merely thought them? He wished he hadn't had so much to drink.

Allan lifted his head and blinked in the glare. The heat was suffocating, and his pale skin felt scorched already. Heat waves undulated from the ground, blurring the horizon and the land into a haze of smudgy blues, whites, and browns. Allan's fingers clawed into the dust beneath him, and particles jammed up under his nails. Slowly his eyes focused on the golden terrain, blazing under a hot sun.

It wasn't dust. It was sand; very fine sand, nearly a powder. He'd landed right smack dab in the middle of a desert, from the looks of things. The sun—*it has to be a sun, right? I can't look at it directly*—sat high above at its blistering noonday zenith.

"Jordan," he croaked, and received another choking mouthful of sand for his trouble. The sand was so fine it responded to the lightest of breezes, including an inhalation from a desperate mouth mere inches away.

He coughed and spat, then rolled onto his back. His joints creaked from the zap through time and space. The portal was gone. Nothing remained except a charred black stripe in the sand where it had opened. Wait, there was something. Allan reached for a stone that was flashing, stealing the sunlight and shooting it into Allan's eyes like a mirror. His fingers closed around the small hard rock, and he cried out at the heat of it and dropped it.

Desert glass? Has it always been here, or was it created when the portal opened? And where are the bugs? He cast about for the small bodies, watching for glints of light, but there was nothing but dunes and corn-colored sand stretching out into infinity in soft, almost elegant drifts. The terrain looked as though an endlessly moving sea had caressed it, pulling back and forth and lifting it into peaks.

Allan slowly stood, dusting sand from his clothing and skin and double-checking all his organs and limbs. Best to make sure he hadn't lost something during his interstellar journey. His dress shoes sank into the hot sand, and the fine powder filled them, making them heavy. He raised a hand and shielded his eyes from the sun. It didn't help much. Sweat had soaked through his shirt already. The air was hot as an oven, and Allan's tongue and lips already felt dry and swollen. There was nothing in sight.

No, wait. He could see a range of cracked, dark mountains rearing on the horizon. Allan cursed softly. He'd come through in a drunken state with heroism in his mind. Now he was here, wherever *here* was, and there was no sign of Jordan. Or water. Or anything else, for that matter. Nothing but inhospitable desert.

Allan cast around for anything of use, but not even the empty bourbon bottle appeared to have survived the journey. He stripped off his shirt, ripped off his undershirt, and put his button-up back on. He folded the white undershirt into one long piece of fabric then wrapped it around his forehead in a makeshift turban, tucking the ends up underneath. It helped cut down some of the sun's glaring heat, but not all. At least it would keep any sweat from dripping into his eyes.

He felt the sun baking the skin on his neck, his lips, and the backs of his hands. Allan had always burned rather than tanned; it was Jaclyn who had given her beautiful olive complexion to Jordan. This adventure wouldn't end well, he could tell already.

"No use sticking around," he said to himself with a chin-wobbling chuckle. This was one of those situations where if he didn't laugh, he would cry. He had to find water. *Deserts have oases, right? Hopefully, this desert is like the ones back on Earth.* Nerves erupted at that thought. Earth. He wasn't on Earth anymore. He was somewhere else, and he couldn't have named it if he tried. He bent and picked up a handful of the yellow sand, letting it trickle through his fingers. It was picked up by the gentle breeze, and drifted away like a haze of flour.

He took the first step away from the black skid mark and the desert glass, and then the second. He put his arm up to block the strange, snaking wind, which picked up suddenly and blasted the sand against him. The sting made his chest itch, but he didn't stop. He surveyed the lay of the land and–

The sand exploded in front of him. Four shapes rose from the ground, two short enough to be children.

Allan stumbled back, palms out, gasping in surprise. His heart tripped and hammered. He froze, his eyes widening at the creatures who had popped out of the desert sand like daisies.

Two men, yes, with dreadlocks and skin like crocodile leather. Goggles hid their eyes behind blackened, dusty lenses, and they grinned at him, yellow-toothed. But they weren't what drew his attention.

If Allan's heart had pounded any harder, it might have plopped right out of his chest and landed on the sand.

The smaller shapes weren't children. They were rats. Silver rats with too much skin. Walking on their hind legs rats. No, one was down on all fours, and they were naked except for a tiny loincloth and a belt which held it in place. The standing rat wore an eyepatch and rubbed his paws together, looking at Allan with a keen eye. A hungry eye.

"This one used a portal, yes?" the rat asked his companions.

Holy crap, did the rat just speak? Allan's mouth opened and shut, and a trembling hand fluttered to his mouth like a lady with a fan. He searched for words, but all that came to his mind was *'talking rat'*. If his skin could've crawled right off his body, it would have. Suddenly, the scalding sun and endless, empty desert didn't seem so bad.

"Quiet, Willen," one of the men said. The tallest one, with the yellowest teeth, bore more than a passing resemblance to a rat himself.

The silver rat drew himself up as straight as he could, then pawed at the folds of skin that covered his sides and drew out a gold talisman.

Allan blinked, shocked sober. "I come in p-peace," he finally said. *That is what one says when faced with aliens, right? Or as an alien, rather...*

"You come in pieces, if we decide so," another man said, this one shorter than the first, with a back as broad as he was tall, and muscled like a workhorse. The rough terrain of his dried-out skin seemed to reflect the sun in patches.

"Bo, you don't speak with him," the first guy said. "I speak with him."

Bo pursed his thick, dusty lips and then snarled like a dog, spittle spraying onto his chin.

The rats actually chuckled, looking at one another. It was a strange sound—a high-pitched sort of purr, accompanied by a gnashing of their sharp front teeth.

"Look at the gypsies, yes? Look how they argue." The rat on all fours pawed at the hot sand, throwing it up like it was confetti.

This is madness, Allan thought. Please tell me Jordan did not fall into these creatures' paws. 'Gypsies' was a term he recognized. The gypsies back home were trinket collectors and nomads. Perhaps these folk would be the same. "I don't mean any harm," Allan said in a calm soothing tone.

"He don't mean harm," the man called Bo sneered, and whipped off his thick goggles, one eye pointed inward at the bridge of his nose. "He don't mean harm, Kam." He chuckled.

Kam, the tall one, snorted. "Harm found you, portal hopper. You hop portals all the time, do you?"

The standing rat shook his golden talisman, and then pointed a long thin claw toward the mountain range in the distance. "Long ways to go yet. We find the stash, we leave him behind, yes?"

"No," Kam growled.

Allan pushed his hands outward in what he hoped counted as a gesture of supplication. "I'm not a… portal hopper, as you call it. I came here by accident. I don't want to cause any trouble. You can understand that, surely, fine men and–uh–rats, such as yourselves. I'm sure you've seen your fair share of trouble in the past." He went for a charismatic grin but it translated as a rictus of fear.

"This one talks too much. Cut out his tongue, yes?" the

standing rat suggested. Then his expression changed, and he seemed to think better of it. He shook the trinket again. "No time, no time, though. We must go."

"Wait." The sitting rat rose onto his hind legs, pink nose probing the air. "He smell like good meat."

"We no eat no men," Bo grunted. "We say so already, too many times. Rats don't listen."

Kam socked his comrade on the arm. "We no eat no man," he agreed then gave a "Ha!"

"Then what to do with him?"

The four surreal characters tapped their chins or snouts and sniffed the air. They huddled closer together while Allan stood statue-like. *I could run while they talk, but to where? The mountain is miles away. They'd be on me in moments. They look like they live out here; this is their territory.*

Allan found himself hoping they might be able to help him. Though the whole 'good meat' thing wasn't a promising sign. He cleared his throat, thinking he'd try for some empathy. "Do you have families? Sons? Daughters?"

The group ignored him. "Portal hopping illegal," one of the rats said for the second or third time. He scratched underneath his eyepatch. "Warden pay good gold for him. Maybe more than what we find at mountain stash."

"Warden one day walk from here," Kam replied. "We no walk a day for bad pay. We go to mountain."

"We go to mountain, he die, we have good meat, yes?" The rat with the eyepatch brightened, hopeful that his companions might change their minds about having man for dinner.

"We no eat no man." Bo folded his muscly arms across his open leather vest. His sand-coated goggles sat on top of his dreadlocks like a bulbous second set of eyes.

The men and rats descended into a flurry of ill-spoken protests and arguments. Allan could barely keep track, and looked from one to the other while they decided his fate.

Allan tried again. "I've lost my daughter. Have you seen—" then he second-guessed himself. Maybe telling this horde of degenerates about Jordan would be a bad idea. He closed his mouth, but none of them acknowledged that he'd spoken. Allan's mind raced for a way out of the situation. He looked down at his Rolex, thinking.

Finally, the rat with two healthy beady eyes flashed a look at Allan, then back to his companions. "Warden not a day, only four hour walk from here," he said. His snout gave a jerk, like a punctuation mark after his statement.

"Why you no say before?" Kam raised a meaty fist, but the rat glared at him, and Kam lowered it slowly with a frown. He wouldn't strike the rat. *Interesting*, thought Allan. *These four seem like uneasy business partners. Perhaps I can take advantage of that.*

"If not for the meat, then for the money," the rat said coldly.

"I'm sure we can come to some sort of agreement that doesn't involve ransom or... or cannibalism," Allan said, then added, "or the warden," as an afterthought. If using a portal was illegal, he didn't want to know what this warden fellow would do about it. Did they have prisons here? "You see, where I'm from, I am an excellent spokesperson and negotiator. You seem in a desperate way; perhaps I can help improve your positions. We can help each other."

"Too much talk!" Bo pressed his palms to his ears.

"You cut out the tongue," one-eyed rat said. "He don't need his tongue for the warden. Also tongue is nice, very tasty."

"Stop with the talk-talk," Kam shook his head. "Too much long words."

Allan swallowed. "I can help you, is what I'm saying," he continued. "I know ways to get things done that others don't. I'm experienced in diplomacy; perhaps I can help negotiate on behalf of your people. I can be very helpful—" Allan listened to himself and cringed inside. *I sound like a desperate fool.* He clenched his eyes tight with frustration. *I am a desperate fool.*

"What's this 'diplomacy'?" the one-eyed rat snapped.

"Type of fish?" Kam shrugged.

"No, it's—" Allan stuttered weakly. This situation was completely out of control and rapidly heading south. There was nothing in all his years of political experience that had prepared him to face two bloodthirsty talking rats and two steampunk gypsies with snakeskin.

"We no want no fish," Bo said. "We need gold." He tapped a golden front tooth. "Dipolmacee taste bad to me."

"The warden we come." Kam marched forward and grabbed Allan's hands. He jerked them behind his back, and cold metal looped across his wrists.

Allan shuddered. "No, please. Please, listen to m—"

There was a terrific *crack*, and pain blasted through the back of Allan's head. He careened forward, unconscious before even hitting the desert floor.

* * *

A<small>LLAN BECAME</small> conscious first of the driving pain in the back of his head, and then of the sensation of cool humid air, and the sound of waves crashing onto a beach. Slowly, memory returned to him. Talking rats. Ignorant, muscular men covered in pale sand and wearing dusty goggles. A negotiation that went so poorly it had ended with a crack of something hard across his skull. The oak tree. The bugs… had he dreamed them? Allan's eyes cracked open. His mouth felt dry and thick, like it was coated with sawdust. He blinked and stretched an arm up over his head. "Ow," he said as his knuckles scraped against something rough and hard. A stone wall. He pushed himself to sitting, rubbing his hand and then the back of his head. He winced at the tender lump there.

His bed was nothing but planks of wood balanced on concrete blocks. Sunlight streamed into the space from a slatted narrow window high above his head, and the light hit the floor in stripes. *Stripes?* Allan looked up, his hand still cradling his poor head. There were bars on the window. Allan rubbed his eyes and looked around properly. Cold dread poured into his gut like ice water, and he fought to quell the panic rising in his breast. He was in a small but very tall cell, with a single low door that had a single low slatted window. The cry of gulls made him cock his head, and he closed his eyes as a fresh breeze of sea air swept through.

Allan got up and climbed up onto his sleeping pallet. The window was still too high for him to peer out of, but he hooked his fingers over the ledge and gave a short jump. Locking his arms, elbows bracing against the stone wall, Allan was able to get a view. His prison was not far up a grassy slope covered in sand the same color as in the desert he'd ported to. Long grasses swayed in the wind coming off the water, and dark waves broke along a pebbly beach. Allan just caught sight of a rickety-looking gray dock standing on posts and jutting out into the waves. There was no living soul in sight, save for the sea birds that screamed and dove into the waves.

The sound of a door slamming made Allan release his grip and drop back onto the pallet. He scooted off the bed and went to crouch at the door and peer through the bars. A plate with a few dry crusts of bread on it and a cracked tin cup half-filled with water were sitting just inside the door. Allan sniffed the water and darted out his tongue to taste it. Satisfied that it was fresh water, he drank it all at once. He peered out through the bars. Only the sight of another cell door greeted him.

"Hello?" he called out into the dark hallway.

"Bonjour," answered a dry, grating voice in the cell across from Allan. Something moved, making a sort of heavy slithering bump. Allan trained his eyes on the small barred window in the door. A face appeared, a man's face with big pockets of fat under his eyes and a thick grizzled beard. "You sound American," said the man, squinting across the hall at Allan.

"You sound French," replied Allan. He wrapped his fingers around the bars of the window and then snatched them back when he felt that they were as cold as ice.

"French I am and French I'll stay," said the man, his accent thick and soothing to the ears in spite of his raspy voice. "Until my dying day." He gave a throaty chuckle, which transformed into a deep chest cough.

"You don't sound so well," said Allan.

"I earned it." The man thumped his chest and gave another cough. "I like the tobacco."

"Ah." Allan could relate. He liked the bourbon. "I wondered if you might tell me where we are?"

"Vischer," replied the man, peering at Allan through the bars. His gray eyes looked weary but intelligent. "The butthole of the Saour Desert, where it shits you out into this miserable sea." His head jerked sideways in the direction of the water. "This is a pisse-froid endroit oublié. Nothing but a cooler for living slabs of meat. There is nothing on these coasts for hundreds of miles. Nothing but stupid gypsies and stinking rats and oiseaux démon."

"Where are you from?"

"Je suis de Paris. Et toi?"

Allan gaped at the face across the hall. "You're from *Paris*? How did you end up here? In this... universe?"

"Ah," the man sighed dramatically. "That is a very long story. To make a very long story a very short story, I was caught importing Pont l'Evêque without the paperwork, and..." Dirty fingers poked through the bars and waved meekly, "here I am."

"You're here for importing *French cheese*?"

The man nodded. "Oui. I will not be here long. That caca boudin Jenner, if he has sent my letter to Operyn how I asked, I have powerful friends who will make miserable his life. Such a waste." He sighed again. "These Oriceran laws are made by idiots."

"Oriceran?"

The finger tapped on the window ledge. "This place. Where we are." An eyeball pulled closer to the space between the bars. "Et toi? D'ou êtes-vous?"

"I am from Virginia. I'm Allan." He brought his face closer to the bars so the man could see him better. "Allan Kacy. Enchanté," he added with a weak smile.

"Marceau." The eyes bobbed as the man nodded. "It is a sad thing to meet you here, mon ami."

"Enough words!" Bellowed a loud voice from the end of the hall. The sound of a door banging against a wall made Allan jump, and Marceau narrowed his eyes in the direction of the noise.

"Je te chie dans le cou!" Marceau yelled down the hall with his mouth to the bars. He gave a coughing laugh at his own insult and squinted at Allan. "He understands no French. L'idiot."

Loud thumping steps drew near, and a pair of legs stopped in front of Marceau's cell. A wooden baton cracked against the bars. Marceau snatched his fingers back just in time.

"Shut your face, cheese-man."

The legs took a few steps toward Allan's cell, and a face appeared, pockmarked and scarred. The guard scratched his cheek with blunt fingers as he peered at Allan. "Awake?" A cloud of foul breath assaulted Allan's nose, and he jerked his face back. The guard produced a set of keys and rattled away with them in the lock. "Out!" He belted as the short door swung open.

Allan crouched and went through the door, standing to face his captor. The brute clamped iron chains around Allan's wrists and shoved Allan down the hall ahead of him. Marceau's face appeared in the bars, his eyes full of sympathy. According to Marceau, he had friends in high places and wouldn't be in here long. Allan had no such friends and didn't know where he was or exactly why he was in prison. If the gypsies were to be believed, it was for falling through a portal. Allan had claimed it was accidental, but that wasn't entirely true. He'd seen the messenger bugs clear the way from one universe into another, and he'd stepped through with the understanding that he was passing through some kind of interdimensional door. What he hadn't known was that anyone considered it illegal. *Surely that's worth something?*

Allan found himself ungraciously shoved through the door at the end of the hall, and plunked on a hard wooden chair in front of a small desk—behind which sat a small balding man with a red face.

"Unlock him," said the balding man without so much as a glance at Allan.

With a grunt, the guard took the chains from Allan's wrist. "I'm right behind you," the guard breathed the words into Allan's face. Allan turned his nose to the side and couldn't help but make a face of disgust at the man's reeking breath. It smelled like every tooth he had was rotting in his head. A hand grabbed Allan's jaw and straightened his face so the two men were eye to eye. "Give us a kiss." He made a smacking sound.

"That's enough, Wilmot," said the balding man, clearly the superior here. The guard gave one last smack into Allan's face and then moved to stand behind him.

The balding man finally graced Allan with a look. Allan shivered. They were cold, dead eyes, void of feeling—even void of that shine of life, for they were dull, colorless. "Do you understand why you are here?"

Allan considered his jailer. *How to approach this?* He felt instinctively that the man would not respond well to weakness. Allan himself was in a place of power back home; if all that time spent making authoritative speeches wouldn't help now, what good was he? "I understand," began Allan, forcing strength into his voice that he didn't really feel, "that I was accosted by criminals in the desert, assaulted, and brought here against my will and under duress." Allan kept his voice calm and his eyes on the man's face. "I suspect that wild accusations were likely made by my captors while I was unconscious and unable to defend myself, and that, in all likelihood, money was exchanged for my person. Do I have any of that wrong?"

The man across the desk was unmoved throughout this speech. He did not react, he did not melt. The only change was a slight lifting of the upper lip, an expression Allan recognized as disdain. Allan's heart fell. That expression belied a lack of respect that was critical for negotiation. The man leaned forward, his eyes penetrating. "Do you deny illegally using a portal to pass from Earth to Oriceran?"

Allan's lips parted and he hesitated. Did he tell the truth here, or did he lie only to get caught out later? He had no idea how to confound anyone into thinking he was native here. "No, I do not deny using a portal. But I do deny having any knowledge of it being illegal. If I had known that—"

"Ignorance is no defense," the man replied dismissively. He grabbed a large wooden stamp and pounded it on the page in front of him. He picked up a quill and wrote something on the bottom of the document with a flourish. "Thank you for your full confession." He picked up the page, folded it and handed it to Wilmot, who snatched it with a grunt and shoved it into a pocket inside his coat. The balding man waved a hand, and Wilmot grabbed Allan under the arm.

"Wait, now what?" Allan said. His voice cracked, and he felt all his bravado fall away.

"Now you go where all portal jumpers go," grunted Wilmot.

"Yes," murmured the balding man, looking down and shuffling through the papers and books on his desk, in search of something. "As soon as I can arrange some blasted transport—"

"Where is that?"

"Trevilsom Prison," Wilmot sneered into Allan's face as he dragged him from the office.

"Wait! Please don't do this," Allan pleaded, kicking the door as Wilmot dragged him through it and back toward his cell. "My daughter. I need to find my daughter!" His cries echoed down the hall, bringing Marceau back to the bars on his window.

Allan found himself unceremoniously dumped back in his cell, and the door locked behind him.

CHAPTER 7

The Arpaks spread their wings and climbed from the platform on the water. Just as they took off, a huge gust of wind blasted them from beneath, catching their wings like a parachute snapping open and hurtling them into the sky.

"Wooo hoooo!" Jordan startled with a laughing scream. "What was that?" She was clutching Blue, who'd squirmed in surprise at the sudden velocity.

Sol laughed at Jordan's reaction. "Courtesy of the Republic of Rodania, a little send-off to help its winged citizens and guests make their way home." Sol did a spiral in the air beside Jordan, grinning and curling his wings tight around him like a bullet, only to snap them open again. *Man, it feels so good to be home.* He was enjoying showing Jordan his home more than he thought he would. It was fun to introduce an uninitiated to the beauty of his city.

"Hey!" Jordan's voice called behind him.

At first Sol thought she was calling after him to wait for her, but as he peered back through his toes, it seemed Blue had wriggled himself free of Jordan's grasp and was flapping and twisting, almost as though he was trying to mimic Sol's movements.

"Blue!" Jordan cried out, trying to snatch the small blue reptile as he struggled to right himself. Her voice was full of terror, and Sol's own heart leapt into his throat as he watched the dragon flail. If he fell, Sol might be able catch him before he hit the waves below—but then again he might not, and from this height, the water would be as hard as concrete.

Blue gave a screech and righted himself, his sapphire wings opening out and catching the updraft. Suddenly he was airborne, and keeping up with Jordan. His strokes were awkward at first, but quickly became smooth and mechanical. The dragon gave a happy whistle and looked at Jordan. Sol thought Blue was grinning; his red slender tongue hanging out like a limp thread, and his needle-sharp teeth gleaming in the evening sunlight.

"Blue!" Jordan said again, but this time with the raptured delight of a mother whose child had just taken his first tottering steps. "You're flying! Oh, good boy, Blue! You're amazing!"

Blue gave another whistle and made a large proud helix around Jordan to celebrate. Jordan's delighted laugh filled the skies, and Sol grinned again, his heart threatening unexpectedly to burst with joy. *How has this girl come to mean so much to me so fast?* He swallowed down the lump of fear in his throat. Sol was a loner, a traveller, an emissary of King and Council. He had important work to do. Loving someone had always seemed like a distraction; a complication he could do without and, based on many of the marriages and relationships he'd seen crumble around him in his lifetime, a downright bad idea.

Jordan, oblivious to all of the thoughts Sol was having, flashed him a grin and jabbed a thumb at Blue. Her smile faltered when thoughts of her father materialized, as they were wont to do in the midst of any happy moment. *Is Allan okay? What did he do after receiving my message? Was he alone when he received it?* As soon as Jordan found Jaclyn, Allan would be next on her list. She would have her family whole and together again, or die trying.

Upper Rodania loomed overhead as they climbed on drafts of

warm air. A ceiling of puffy white drew closer. Sol changed course to fly parallel to the underside of the island.

"This way," he called, skimming the dark spikes of earth jutting from the fog. "Keep close." Taking a long, curving turn, Sol flew straight at a patch of swirling cloud and vanished.

"Sol?" Jordan's heart triple-flipped as she lost sight of him. The fog closed in around her; the only evidence of Sol's passage were the whorls and fog-devils he'd left behind. Her skin grew cool and she slowed her speed, unable to see beyond the fog in front of her face. "Sol?" she called a second time. Blue tucked in tight beside her, flapping steadily near her abdomen. He gave an uncertain croak at the thick haze they found themselves in.

"Keep climbing!" came Sol's voice from right on top of her. "Nearly there!" His voice was so close it made her pull up and gasp, feeling like she might get kicked in the face accidentally if she wasn't careful.

An explosion of white light made her eyes squeeze shut. She opened them, blinking rapidly as they adjusted. Blue gave a piercing cry of excitement. The hazy brightness cleared as the two Arpaks and the small dragon exploded from a swirling pool of cloud and flew up through the center of Upper Rodania. Passing first gardens and trees, then skimming ivy-covered stone towers, and cliffs dripping with foliage, they were but tiny sparrows against a colossal urban backdrop.

Jordan's jaw dropped at the beauty around her—the wealth, the abundance, the singular architecture; most of all, the citizens. The air was chaotic with Strix, magnificent winged men and women making their way this way and that, some with armloads of items, some flying with a companion and deep in discussion as they kept a lazy pace, their wings matching each other's, stride for stride.

No one so much as blinked at their presence.

"You have highways!" Jordan noted with surprise. The flying

Strix kept to a semi-organized flow, going only East on this plane, and only West on that one. "And the *colors!*"

Many of the Strix were earthy in their coloring, but Jordan was thrilled to see that there were nearly as many Arpaks with bright green, blue, even pink and purple feathers. She fit right in with her bright canary yellow plumage. It seemed that for every Arpak with brightly colored wings, there was a matching tropical bird on Earth. The Nychts were nearly always black, dark gray, light gray, or some shade of brown, from deep chocolate to taupe. Skin tones of both Arpaks and Nychts were as varied as any on Earth—from porcelain to midnight—and there didn't seem to be any correlation between skin tone and wing type.

But there was something that tied them all together—every Nycht looked tired, and like they were on a serious mission to somewhere. In contrast, the Arpaks mostly looked pink-cheeked; several looked downright jolly.

They flew by outdoor terraces and landing platforms lined with columns and arches that led through to semi-open spaces filled with interesting furniture. Towers constructed of every material, from granite to marble to all colors of dull metal, stretched up towards the sky and were stacked with platforms and windows. Flowers and vines wrapped around everything and spilled from everywhere.

"It's marvelous," Jordan said, nearly breathless. "I have never seen anything like it."

"I should think not," Sol replied as they joined the flow of sparse traffic cruising through turrets and spires. "There is nowhere else like it, on Earth or on Oriceran."

"Are we going to your place?" It had been a very long several days of traveling, and Jordan felt an ache deep in her back that wouldn't go away without a long sleep.

"The palace, actually. I need to deliver this to Juer as quickly as possible." He patted the satchel at his hip.

"The palace," Jordan whispered. She had to be in a dream. At any moment she could wake up, and all of this would vanish.

But she didn't wake, and it didn't vanish.

Her mom was here somewhere—that was the craziest part of all of this.

"Can we ask about my mother?"

"Of course," Sol replied. "I'll take you to the public offices on Middle Rodania. Registration information is stored there. As long as she gave her Earth name when she first entered Rodania, she'll be in the system."

"Right." Jordan blinked at the unexpected and unwelcome idea that Jaclyn might have changed her name. Her mind began to shuffle through reasons why she might do such a thing, and she gasped as a terrace loomed abruptly in front of her. She had to bank suddenly to avoid it.

Sol led them over what seemed like endless gardens, parks, and buildings. Jordan spotted other non-winged species on various platforms—the occasional Elf, and what could be Dwarves or even Leprechauns, Jordan didn't know—sitting under arches, around tables, discussing whatever needed to be discussed in Strix society. Everyone seemed to be dressed in fine clothing, with their hair nicely coiffed.

Traffic thinned as they curved upward, and the spires grew further and further apart. More space had been allotted for parks. Large waterfalls spilled over rock walls, sparkling water coursed endlessly and twinkled in the sun. Rivers and lakes snaked and pooled across the rolling landscape and Arpaks could be seen strolling leisurely, swimming, or lolling on the grass and reading. The land was so extensive that Upper Rodania didn't feel like an island at all.

They arrived at the uppermost spire constructed of something that looked an awful lot like mother-of-pearl; it swirled with all the colors of the rainbow against a background of sunset.

Blue bumped against Jordan's stomach and gave a plaintive

squeak. Jordan looked down and saw the way he was laboring. She put her arms out. The dragon cozied up to her, and she took his weight. He closed his wings and huffed out a sigh.

"Getting tired?" she asked. "It's been a big day for you. Your first day flying."

"What was that?" Sol called back.

"Nothing. Just talking to Blue." As they approached the palace, Jordan noted that Sol already looked more serious. They landed on a platform and settled their wings.

A large terrace of white stone spread before them, decorated with a pergola choked with vines. A long table and benches sat under the sheltering greenery, awaiting some large party of importance. Beyond, in a recess carved into the pearly wall, a fountain splashed from a tap and landed in a basin. They drank and refreshed themselves. Jordan steadied Blue on the edge of the basin, keeping him from splashing headfirst into the pool while he stuck his face entirely beneath the surface and took long sucks of water.

"Do you mind waiting while I find Juer and make the delivery? I shouldn't be long. Help yourself to some fruit." Sol gestured to a bowl on the table that was overflowing.

"No problem. We'll be here." Jordan's mouth began to water at the idea of food. They hadn't eaten since Maticaw. Flying burned a lot of calories, and her stomach grumbled that it knew it.

Sol strode towards the open, towering entrance to a space seemingly filled with nothing but columns. He turned back. "You'll be here when I get back, right?"

"I'll be here." To show she meant business, Jordan pulled out one of the chairs at the end of the long table, plopped herself into it, and threw a leg up on the table. Blue hopped into her lap and tucked his head under his wing.

Sol nodded and disappeared into the labyrinth of marble.

Jordan closed her eyes and tilted her head back. Stroking Blue's scales calmed her, and her heart finally slowed its frenetic pace from the long climb. She opened her eyes and spotted a small pink fruit on the top of the pile. She hooked a finger over the edge of the wooden bowl and pulled it toward herself. She picked up the pink fruit and sniffed it. Sweet like a plum. She took a bite and groaned with pleasure as the juice rolled over her tongue. Very plumlike, but with a slightly bitter aftertaste.

Blue let out a clicking purr and took his head out from under his wing to sniff at the fruit.

"Want to try it?" Jordan bit off a chunk and held it for Blue to take. He bumped his little nose against it a few times, and his tongue snaked out for a lick, but he didn't eat it.

"Not convinced, huh? We didn't have time to discuss dietary needs with the gypsy lady," Jordan recalled. "What do you like to eat?"

Blue just gazed at her, and then settled his chin on her forearm while she finished the pink plum and reached for a second.

Blue's head jerked up as she was biting into her third plum, and he peered over her arm intently as though he'd spotted something in the bushes near the basin. His tongue snaked out again, and he cocked his head.

"What is it, boy?"

His body tensed, he hopped onto the table and lowered his head, nose pointed at the bush the way a pointer shows the location of a bird. He froze there like a stone gargoyle.

Jordan sat mute and fascinated, watching. For a moment it seemed the two of them were statues rather than blood and bone.

Blue darted across the table, head low and spine curving in a serpentine fashion. At the edge of the table, he made a silent leap. His wings opened for a short glide across the grass before pinning against his sides. He disappeared into the leaves, and Jordan got up, the plum forgotten, dripping juice in her hand.

"Blue?"

The leaves shook and rattled with some silent struggle, and

Blue emerged with a large brown lump of fur in his jaws. He almost tottered forward onto his face from the weight of it.

"Wow!" Jordan exclaimed. "That thing is almost as big as you are." The lump had a short skinny tail, which was limp and dangling. "At least you're a fast killer. I used to hate seeing the way our barn cats would play with their kills." Blue made an effortful leap back onto the table with his prize, dripping bight droplets of blood as he marched proudly up to Jordan. Jordan's stomach rolled forward and she put what was left of the pink plum down. "Good boy, Blue. I think. Uh-" she scooped up the dragon and his meal and set him on the stones underneath the table. "Maybe not on the table."

Blue promptly began to snack on the rodent, which Jordan didn't really feel like inspecting more closely. She cleaned up the blood with leaves taken from nearby shrubs, and wandered to the platform's edge where she could enjoy the view of Upper Rodania without hearing the crunch of breaking bones.

CHAPTER 8

The sound of a footstep made Jordan turn. Sol strode out from under the arches wearing a wrinkle of worry between his brows.

"What's wrong?" Jordan asked.

"Juer isn't here. Which is a bit weird; he lives here now. He moved to the palace over a year ago."

"Was there anyone else around who knows where he went?"

"I was told to try his old place on Middle. I thought he sold that place a long time ago, or at least rented it out." He came to stand beside Jordan at the edge of the terrace. "Where's Blue?"

Jordan pointed under the table, where Blue was curled up like a cat and chewing on the last of the rodent he'd killed. A piece of red flesh disappeared between his chops, and he perked up his head and looked up at the Arpaks now staring at him.

"What is he eating?"

"Hopefully not anyone's pet," said Jordan. "He killed a rodent."

"Really? I thought Miniatures were mostly herbivores," Sol mused as they went over to the table and peered under at the reptile.

"He sure wasn't interested in that pink plum I ate." Jordan

watched as Blue stretched and got to his feet. "You ate everything! Even the bones. How practical and efficient you are."

Blue whistled and waddled out from under the table with a fat belly. The yellow scales on the sides of his gut stretched apart to accommodate for his meal.

"Are you going to be able to fly?" Jordan asked, watching Blue totter up to her foot.

As though in answer, Blue spread his leathery blue wings and flapped laboriously into the air, swaying weightily.

"Alright, then. On to Middle Rodania," said Sol, straightening. "Good thing it's below us."

The Arpaks dove from the terrace with Blue following, and Sol led as they spiraled over the palace park and wove through spires and towers to the edge of Upper Rodania. They dropped over the edge like logs over a waterfall, and this time Jordan remembered to close her nictitating membranes against the *whoosh* of air in her face. She couldn't help but give a whoop as her stomach got left behind.

Middle Rodania grew large at an alarming rate and the Arpaks put on the brakes after their face-first freefall. Jordan's heart pounded happily in her chest and she marvelled at how only a short time ago, she'd been sitting on the chair under her oak, completely unwitting of her true self. The anxiety that rose up whenever she thought of her human life and all the things left unresolved threatened her with panic, and she shoved the worries into some small dark corner to deal with later.

Middle Rodania was beautiful, but in a less opulent way than Upper. Stretched out before them was a verdant green landscape dotted with villages, roads and lakes. The hills and valleys transformed into lush forested land, with the spires of tall structures—homes, Jordan assumed—thrusting their rooftops up through the thick canopy of leaves. Bells rang in the distance, and Jordan wondered if someone was perhaps getting married, or if the Strix society attended some kind of religious gatherings.

The forest melted into a more densely populated area, and a marvelous city of stone structures, spires, and ceramic rooftops opened up below them. A sparkling river snaked its way through the ancient-looking metropolis, crisscrossed with bridges clearly built for the non-flying citizens of Rodania.

The Arpaks slowed as they passed over the city. Jordan followed Sol as he drifted lower and banked to where an unusual skyline of buildings interrupted the bustling throughways of the roads and rivers. The tall towers of stacked platforms, which by now seemed to be typical of Rodanian architecture, clustered in one area like any earthly inner city. *The downtown core*, thought Jordan. Layers upon layers of crisscrossing roads and bridges hanging in the air tied the towers together, and beings of all kinds moved tirelessly along these arteries like blood cells.

Jordan followed Sol straight down into this network of activity, and the flying became tighter and much slower, their wingstrokes becoming more frequent as the wind died down. Sol landed on a gray stone platform and held out a hand for Jordan. Jordan took it as her boots skimmed over the stones and her wings closed up gracefully. Blue, however, came flying in too fast and rolled like a bowling ball over the dusty stones, snout over tail, wings flopping uselessly. He bumped up against a wooden door, which opened inward. With a surprised squeak, the bloated dragon flopped backwards into the shop.

"My word," squealed an elderly Arpak woman with tiny, dove-gray wings, the tips of which barely reached her knees. She hopped nimbly over the reptile, moving with far more grace than one would expect from an elderly person. She smiled at Sol and Jordan, her white hair a fluff of cloud around her head. A thousand wrinkles sprang to life on her face, and she pointed at Blue. "There's something you don't see every day. Glad I didn't squash him!" And with that, she dropped over the side of the platform and out of sight. Jordan gasped, but the woman's undersized wings did open and she swooped up and away.

Blue waddled out of the shop, his blue scales muted with dust. He gave a sneeze and wandered up to Jordan where he sat and looked up at her sheepishly. Jordan scooped him up and brushed him off until his blue scales gleamed again.

"So, flying right after eating makes you a klutz," she murmured to her reptilian companion. "Duly noted." She lifted him to her shoulder, where he parked himself partly under her hair and blinked drowsily. "Goodness, you're much heavier," noted Jordan as his weight settled into the crook of her neck and shoulder. "That rodent was huge."

"This way," Sol called. He was already halfway down the street and beckoning to Jordan.

Jordan followed, keeping a hand on Blue, whose grip seemed to be a little too relaxed after his meal. She wondered if she should look into getting some kind of backpack made for him so she could carry him whenever he'd had a meal. *Problems for another moment,* she thought, and caught up to Sol.

* * *

"Could we ask Juer if he has seen my mom?" asked Jordan as they wove along the street. "We can show him this," she added, pulling the locket out from under her vest and dangling it where Sol could see.

"Yes, of course we can." Sol had forgotten they had a portrait of Jaclyn. That was helpful.

They turned down an alley filled with shops and buzzing with people going about their business. Sol stopped at a wide wooden door.

"Want me to wait outside?" Jordan asked, catching Blue as he nearly dropped off her shoulder in torpor of sleep and digestion.

"No," Sol smiled at her. "Why don't you come in? Juer works for the king, but he's not royalty and doesn't care for ceremony."

Jordan shot him a dazzling smile. "Okay!" It was the first time

Jordan was going to meet anyone in Sol's life. "Is there any etiquette I should be aware of?"

"Just be yourself." Sol pushed open the tall door, which was obviously built to accommodate Arpaks with large wingspans, and they stepped into a dimly lit space that smelled of mouldering paper and leather. The ceilings reached up four or five stories in a semi-circular library. Books and scrolls were stacked haphazardly on shelves that no human could ever reach without an impressively tall ladder. A Strix, however, would have no trouble spreading their wings in this huge round space and climbing to wherever they needed to draw from.

The wooden floor was inlaid with red and brown wood in a huge wagon wheel pattern, its spokes reaching out in every direction.

"Cool floor," Jordan said.

"It's a ventilation system," explained Sol. "The brown wood drops away and moves over to allow for wind to come up through the floor and go out through the ceiling."

Jordan looked up and saw a similar pattern in the domed ceiling. "How wonderfully clever!"

"Yes and no," laughed Sol. "You should see what happens to anything not nailed down when it's open. There's a reason they stopped building them."

"It's there to help lift an Arpak to a higher shelf?"

"Precisely. A strong Arpak doesn't need the blast of air, but," Sol lowered his voice, "Juer isn't as young as he used to be."

"Whatever do you mean, lad?" came a grating but jovial voice. It bounced around the circular space as though from a disembodied source.

"Juer?"

A balding head with a corona of thin gray fluff poked out from over a balcony. "You've returned, my lad. Excellent, excellent," Juer chuckled. "And what a pretty guest you bring with you. Hello, there." He waved at Jordan.

"Hello," she called up with a grin and a wave.

"I'll be right down," he began to climb over the balcony.

"Don't trouble yourself, we'll come up," said Sol quickly. Jordan saw why; Juer's wings were thin and missing patches of feathers.

"Oh, please let us come up. I would love to see more of your library," said Jordan.

Juer crossed back over the balcony. "Come up, come up, then." His voice dimmed as he vanished into some recess. "Maybe you can help me find what I'm looking for."

Jordan began to spread her wings but Sol said, "There are stairs. Best not disturb his papers with our drafts."

Jordan put her wings away and followed Sol past the library and onto a stone floor where a wide spiral staircase led to the upper levels. Blue gave a sleepy clicking purr. "Do you want to nap while the adults talk?" Jordan asked him. She set him down at the bottom of the stairs. Blue tottered to a chair piled high with books. He curled up underneath it and tucked his head under his wing with a contented sigh. "You sleep as much as a puppy," Jordan remarked before climbing the stairs.

Jordan and Sol ascended two tall stories, passing a room with a bed that looked like someone had had a nightmare in it. Bedding half spilled onto the floor and more pillows than Jordan could count at a glance were scattered across the mattress and on the floor. A large stone fireplace sat cold and dormant. A thin slash of a window let in just enough light to reveal all the dust motes floating in the air.

At the next level they discovered Juer up to his elbows in open books. Scrolls were spread out around him and held down with rocks. Skulls of species Jordan couldn't identify had been demoted into candle holders, and dripped lumpy wax. A wooden table so large it had to have been built there was cluttered with all kinds of research. A chandelier, lit with warm balls of yellow light from an unknown source, swung over the mess, throwing eerie shadows. The two young Arpaks joined the elder one at the table of disaster.

Juer was bent and wizened, but sprung with vitality all the same. He faced the pair with a wrinkly smile and took a closer look at Jordan. He reached out an arthritic hand.

"Sol, you've been keeping secrets from me, my boy. Who's this delightful canary?"

Jordan had to laugh. It was exactly how she'd thought of herself when she first saw her own near-fluorescent feathers.

"I'm Jordan." She clasped his hand gently, careful not to squeeze too hard. But Juer clutched hers in a firm grip that was surprising in its strength.

"A pleasure, a real pleasure," he said. "What are you doing commiserating with my nephew? You know he's nothing but trouble." He held up a twisted finger. "He'll never settle down, mark my words."

"Juer," Sol said, turning pink.

"Uncle?" Jordan looked at Sol.

"He never told you?" Juer chuckled and moved closer to whisper conspiratorially to Jordan. "He's a little embarrassed."

"That's not true," said Sol, his flush deepening.

"He doesn't want people to think he became the king's courier through nepotism," explained Juer.

Jordan looked at Sol's red face, not sure what to say.

"Bully to that," added Juer with some passion. He clapped a wizened hand on Sol's fleshy shoulder. "Sol was top of his class. Weren't you, lad?"

"Okay, *now* I'm embarrassed," said Sol with exasperation. "Can we talk about something else? What are you doing here, Juer?" Sol asked, gesturing at the messy room. "I thought you were going to sell this place and move everything to the castle to save you the traveling?"

"All in due time, my boy. All in due time," the doctor muttered, patting the table absent-mindedly as though searching for something. "I can still make the journey. And it's good for me, I'll wager." His fingers found a pair of square spectacles with thin wire frames and he propped them on his nose. "Can you imagine the nightmare of moving all of this?" He waved at the library behind them. "These things are old—ancient, some of them."

"You wouldn't have to deal with it," Sol said. "You're a citizen of the palace. There are Strix who can do that for you."

Juer peered over his glasses at Sol. "And would those Strix be of skin or of feather, do you think?" he asked slyly.

" 'Of skin or feather'?" Jordan echoed. She watched Sol as he shifted from one foot to the other, clearly uncomfortable. "Oh, you mean Nycht or Arpak?"

Juer grunted and shuffled some papers in front of him, shoving an open book to the side as though whatever he'd found in it had disappointed him. His eyes dusted Sol's body. "You are not carrying a very large bag." A more serious tone had crept into his voice.

Sol reached for his satchel. "Yes, about that." He retrieved the jar of black liquid and handed it to the doctor.

Juer's eyes widened. "This cannot be all?" He took the jar in his twisted hand.

"I'm afraid so. Cles sent you this, as well." Sol handed him the small yellow envelope.

His fingers trembling just a little, Juer took the envelope and set the jar down on the table. He unfolded the letter and tilted his head to read the words through his glasses. His frown deepened.

"This is not acceptable." Juer ran a withered hand over his mouth and jaw. His patchy wings shook with agitation. "This will not do. Something is amiss." He muttered this while turning away from Jordan and Sol; processing, thinking, talking to himself. "Not good."

"What can I do to help, Juer?" Sol asked.

"There is a shortage of lapita medicine," said Juer. "My stores have dwindled and every order I have sent for from Cles has grown smaller and smaller. And now this," he picked up the tiny jar and shook it. The liquid sloshed. "Something must be done." He peered at Cles's letter. "Cles says he cannot get the raw ingredient. It is not for sale anywhere in Maticaw. He has sent letters as far as Skillen with no success."

"What is the raw ingredient?" asked Jordan.

"Gersher fungus," said Juer. "That is the critical ingredient. The others are there merely to stabilize and emulsify."

"But that grows in Charra-Rae," said Sol with surprise. "There was masses of it. We just came from there."

Jordan nodded. "Baskets and baskets of it are harvested daily. We saw it with our own eyes. It's a brown fungus, with a bright pink top. Right?" She almost added that it was harvested by a host of befuddled workers who'd had their brains gnashwitted by the Elves. Their vacant faces still haunted her thoughts.

Juer stared at the two Arpaks. "That's right," he said. "It's pink on top. Bright, like a chilla-feather. Baskets of it, you say?"

The two Arpaks nodded enthusiastically.

"Then the problem is not the raw ingredient. The problem lies elsewhere."

"Do you want me to go back to Charra-Rae? I'm sure we can buy some fungus directly from them."

Juer considered this. "So many problems with that. The raw ingredient is difficult to process, I don't have the skill. It needs to be done by an experienced apothecary, like Cles. And buying direct will be a bureaucratic nightmare of paperwork. You won't be able to get gersher past the borders without alerting the port authorities." Juer began to pace. "It's also a temporary solution. Inefficient. It won't do." Juer's bright intelligent eyes homed in on Sol.

"What?"

"It's not in your job description, but going through the proper channels will take forever. And we don't have time."

"Tell me," said Sol, stepping forward. "What can I do?"

"Pay a visit to Belshar for me. Learn what you can."

Sol cocked his head at the name. *That rings a vague bell.* "The bureaucrat?"

"He's a trade-master," said Juer. "If it's not a problem with the raw ingredient then it's a problem with trade. Speak to him. If he doesn't know what's happening, he should be made aware. Best we can hope for is something simple." Juer waved a hand. "Someone needs to stamp something or give an approval. There's likely an agreement lying forgotten under a pile of documents somewhere. Happens all the time." He tilted his chin and looked at Sol over his glasses. "Would you do that for me?"

"Of course, Uncle Juer. I have no other commission at the moment. I'll go today. Right now."

"Thank you, my boy." Juer took off his glasses and rubbed the bridge of his nose. "But go tomorrow. The office will be closed by now, and you both look tired."

Sol nodded. "Alright. I'll go first thing." He looked at Jordan. Shall we go home?"

Jordan nodded, she was eager to see where Sol lived. She pulled the locket out from under her vest. "Very quickly, I was wondering..." she opened the locket and held it out for Juer to see its interior. "Have you ever seen this woman?" Her bright eyes scanned the old Arpak's face hopefully.

Juer held the locket open on his palm, in the light where he could peer at the face painted inside. "Beautiful lady," he grunted. "I wish I *had* seen her before."

Jordan's heart deflated. "Thank you, anyway."

"Who is she, my dear?"

"My mother," said Jordan, and her throat constricted.

Juer's bushy gray eyebrows arched. "Ah, yes I can see that now; you have her cheekbones. Different eyes, though."

"Yes," said Jordan.

"You've lost your mother—" Juer began, and then waved a hand. "Nevermind. Tell me later. Later. Go."

Sol and Jordan said goodbye and left the old doctor to his studies.

"I'm sorry," murmured Sol as they stepped out onto the street. "We're just getting started. Don't worry."

"I'm not." Jordan brightened. "Rodania is a big place. It's not like everyone knows everyone."

"No. Not remotely," Sol agreed.

* * *

Sol's place was on the third floor from the top of a high granite tower facing the palace. They landed on his terrace, and Jordan turned to take in the view. "Wow!"

"Like it?" Sol felt unexpectedly timid. He didn't bring guests back to his apartment very often. For some reason, it mattered to him that she liked it there.

"It's spectacular!" The setting sun had cast Upper Rodania in a peach colored glow, softening the hills, valleys, turrets, and spires across from and below them. The palace, an elegant cluster of white columns piercing the clouds, reflected the evening light and seemed aglow. Small blue and yellow lights from lanterns and streetlights twinkled from the buildings and roadsides, speckling and crisscrossing the land. "I've never seen such beauty."

Sol was watching Jordan take in the view. "Me either."

They entered the tall-ceilinged apartment, which was a simple and sparsely furnished three room design. Every door was exceptionally tall and wide, giving the place an airy feeling. Handcrafted wooden furniture was sprinkled about, including a huge four-poster bed which could be seen through the arched doorway leading into the bedroom.

"How do you keep intruders from coming in?" Jordan asked, noting that there was no way of locking up the apartment.

"Rodania doesn't have such problems," answered Sol, opening

his icebox. "The blood you give before you can enter Rodania can also be used to track your movements." His voice came from behind the door as he retrieved a selection of vegetables and fruits. "It's more than enough of a deterrent. The punishment for such a thing would be Trevilsom prison." He closed the door and stood before the wooden countertop. "Nobody wants to go there."

Jordan was eyeing the array of vegetables and the slab of frozen dark pink meat that Sol had pulled out. "What's that?"

"It's feroth," Sol said. "Remember that carcass—"

"Don't remind me," Jordan shuddered at the thought of the gigantic beast she'd fallen against after tumbling head over tail into Oriceran. "Please tell me it tastes better than it smells."

"That was a rotting one," Sol began, but when Jordan's face turned a shade of green, he grabbed a squash from the pile of vegetables. "Want to prep this?"

"Yes, please give me an occupation or I shall be sick." Jordan took the squash and smelled it. "It's sweet!"

Sol handed her a knife. "Slice it in half and take out the seeds. Then we bake it."

"Like squash on Earth," Jordan noted.

They worked side-by-side, preparing their meal. Sol poured them both a glass of wine as they waited for the food to cook in the tile stove. Delicious smells began to fill the small kitchen and the two Arpaks sat on the terrace waiting for the meal.

"Where's Blue?" asked Sol as they watched the first of the stars come out.

"He crawled under your bed," replied Jordan. That made her realize that there was only one bed, which made her cheeks pink. "Uh…speaking of which…"

Sol blinked vacantly, then finally clued in. He swallowed too big of a gulp and almost choked. He wiped his mouth. "I'll sleep on the terrace."

"Where?" Jordan looked around at the sparse furniture.

"I'll snug up with a blanket. Don't worry about me."

"Such a gentleman." Jordan held her wine glass up in a salute. Between her exhaustion and the alcohol, she was feeling a bit furry in the brain. She gazed at the darkening sky where two small but bright orbs had hoisted themselves into the sky. "Two moons! How did I not notice them before?"

But Sol had gone inside. He brought the food out, and the two sat down to their feast of squash and grilled feroth. As they both realized how completely famished they were, they ceased all conversation and tore into their meal with gusto.

They cleaned up in sleepy silence afterward, took turns bathing and then fell into bed, Jordan in the bedroom and Sol on the terrace. Sleep came on swift wings to all three of them.

CHAPTER 9

Sleep didn't come easy for Eohne. There were too many questions elbowing each other in her mind, like anxious passengers on a crowded train. Her messenger bugs *still* hadn't returned, and Sohne's insistence that she remain in the forests of Charra-Rae gnawed at her. Worry skittered through her stomach like cockroaches across a tile floor. She sat up in her bed—a mattress stuffed with chilla leaves, set up in the top loft of her home—and pressed her fingers to her stomach.

"This is stupid," she muttered, and rose. She slipped on her leggings and tunic, then pulled on her supple leather boots. She grabbed her utility belt and climbed down the vine ladder to the floor. She bent and checked the glass bottle she'd left outside the door in case the other bugs returned. The glass bugs inside the jar, exactly thirteen of them, didn't move. Still flat. Still dead. Still nothing from the other half of the group.

Concern exploded into full-blown panic and Eohne wrestled it into submission, taking a deep, juddering breath. "They have to come back," she whispered. "Dead or alive, they have to come back." If the bugs returned, there was a chance they would have some information encoded in the juice inside their bodies; it wasn't until they were all together that she'd be able to read it, though. The bugs weren't so much a dozen separate creatures, as they were one entity tethered together by magic. She walked to the edge of the embankment and sank to the mossy ground, hanging her legs over the edge of the outcropping.

The forest was quiet. The paths that connected the trees glimmered softly in the darkness. Stars twinkled between the leaves overhead, but the two moons of Oriceran had already risen high and passed out of sight. Peaceful.

Eohne inhaled through her nose and exhaled through her mouth in an effort to calm her anxiety. The messenger bugs had to have found Jordan's father. She'd designed them herself, tested each prototype and refined them until she'd produced their current form; the lack of return had nothing to do with the efficacy of the bugs. But no matter how she sliced it, something had gone wrong.

Tink.

There was a single sound from inside the jar. Eohne froze with her fingers halfway to her temples, where a headache was just starting to surface.

Tink-tink. Tink, tink, tink.

She scrambled from the ledge and approached the glass jar. Inside it, messenger bugs crawled, glowing palely in the half light. *These aren't dead. No, they are very much alive and still filled with juice!*

Eohne sucked in a breath, grabbed the jar, and rushed into her lab. The blue-white lights illuminated the space, responding to her presence. She placed the jar on her worktable. The yellow butterflies filled the tall glass cylinder in the far corner with fluttering bright bodies, now as awake as Eohne was.

Carefully, Eohne unscrewed the lid, reached inside, and extracted one of the bugs. She loosed a syringe from her utility belt and inserted the needle into the underside of the bug's belly. Glowing, clear fluid filled the beaker. The message had been delivered, otherwise the juice would still be green—but the fact that the fluid was alight told Eohne that the bugs had brought information back with them, just as she'd been hoping for.

"Data," she whispered, her eyes bright. Data was her favorite thing in the world, aside from maybe a freshly toasted elven gurfle soaking with warm butter. She placed the bug back in the jar. She took a small glass disk, lifted her syringe, and squeezed the plunger, sending the juice onto the disk.

She extended her finger, and then hesitated. *What will I discover about Jordan's life? I hope she forgives the violation...* Taking a breath, Eohne pressed her fingertip to the wet, glowing patch.

Her eyes rolled back as a vision exploded in her mind.

A human male with a narrow, friendly, bespectacled face and red hair knelt in front of an old oak tree. He stretched out his hand, dropped it again, stretched out, dropped it—trying, but failing, to place the messenger bugs in mid-air.

"Hello, Dad," Eohne muttered. "Allan Kacy. You touched the bugs; you weren't supposed to keep them, you silly man." Her mind raced as she watched, making adjustments to the science behind the messenger bugs; calculating how, in the future, she might keep them out of reach of whoever was receiving their message.

A portal formed in front of the man, and he gaped at it. He rose from the ground and—

"Ohhhhh," Eohne breathed. "No. You foolish—"

—stepped through the blue, shimmery expanse. There was a white flash and the vision transformed. Allan on his knees in yellow sand—clearly not anywhere close to Charra-Rae. This was a desert. Eohne's mind continued racing along its rails and filing through the different deserts in Oriceran that she was aware of. Her mind and her mind's eye strained for any distinguishing features. *Sand the color of corn.* Allan's glasses were dusty and he'd wound his shirt around his head to beat off the scorching sun. He looked around, bewildered, lost. He called out for Jordan.

Allan stumbled through the sand, kicking up gold powder in his wake. He halted, a frown forming on his lined face.

"What is it?" Eohne whispered—neither in her lab nor in the desert with him, but somewhere in between. "What happened?"

The sand in front of Jordan's father erupted and four shapes emerged from underneath, their skin tanned to nut brown and leathery, their hair in dreadlocks and beetle eyes glinting behind bronze, thick-rimmed glasses.

"Gypsies," Eohne breathed. "He's fallen through to the Saour Desert."

Allan put out his palms and spoke with a pleading, barely-controlled expression on his face. The gypsies talked, exchanged gap-toothed grins. Smaller shadows, just out of sight but moving like rodents, brushed against the sides of her vision. These had to be Willens—crafty talking rats, and possibly slave-traders.

The vision faded, the data used up.

"No!" Eohne's eyelids flew open. She sucked in ragged gasps of air and braced herself on the workbench. She put a hand to her throat. Panic surged again. *Jordan's father is in grave danger, and she has no idea. In fact, no one knows Allan is in danger except for me. I am now his only hope. If I don't act...*

But how?

The Elves of Charra-Rae were forbidden to leave their forest home without permission. She'd already asked Sohne for permission once and been denied. But she had new information now, important information. Eohne didn't fully understand why Sohne had made Jordan promise she would return to Charra-Rae, but Sohne never did anything without a reason, and her ability to catch glimpses of the future gave her foresight that she didn't often share with her people; not until she needed to. *Sohne wants something from Jordan, otherwise why would it be so important to see her again? Perhaps there is a way I can use this information to secure permission to leave.*

The inventor pushed off the bench, her belt clanking in the

silence that was no longer peaceful, but oppressive. She darted out of the tree and along the shimmering path toward Sohne's house.

Eohne walked up the long, sloping path that led to the top floor of Sohne's home, her heart rocketing around in her chest. The lights were on, which meant Sohne was also struggling with sleep this night. Perhaps the gnashwits haunted her at night, too, or perhaps she was receiving the foresight.

Eohne took a minute to calm herself using a few breathing exercises, then tapped on the arched doorway.

"Come," returned Sohne's gentle voice almost in the same moment. It was as though Sohne knew she was going to visit. She probably did; Eohne never knew what Sohne had foresight about, and Sohne rarely let on.

Eohne pushed through the door and into Sohne's abode. The smell of lilies filled the elegant cone-shaped home. A spiral window at the cone's top displayed the broken canopy of trees high above and the sprinkling of stars in between. Sohne's space was little more than a space for relaxation, sleeping, and private conversations, since Charra-Rae Elves lived most of their lives out of doors.

"What is it?" Sohne asked with her back to Eohne, a brush in-hand and halfway down the long expanse of red hair. She was sitting on the edge of her round bed in an evening gown the color of spring leaves–a light, floaty affair that draped over Sohne's long frame like a cloud. Eohne couldn't fathom the expense of it, let alone the annoyance of trying to sleep in it.

"The messenger bugs came back," Eohne said, forcing herself to speak slowly. If there was one thing Sohne didn't respond well to, it was panic. "Alive. With data."

"And?" Sohne cocked an ear toward her; the hand holding the brush went still.

"Jordan's father has been captured. He followed the bugs into Oriceran and has been captured by gypsies in Saour." She took a breath and hid her trembling hands behind her back. *If Sohne denies me a second time... can I trust that the Elf princess is making the right call? Does she know something? Maybe she knows that Allan is already dead. Or maybe she doesn't know anything and will keep me in Charra-Rae for her own selfish reasons.*

"Saour," echoed Sohne, lowering the brush. "Foolish man."

That was exactly what Eohne had said, but aloud she excused him. "He's an Earthling; he doesn't know any better. And he's lost his only family. Can you blame him for taking the opportunity to cross over when it presented itself?"

"No," agreed Sohne. "He can't be blamed." The eye that Eohne could see drifted shut.

Eohne pushed forward in the silence of Sohne's meditation. "I don't know why you made Jordan promise to return, but she has to be important to you for some reason. And if she's important to you, then her father should be important to you, too."

Sohne didn't respond.

"Do the right thing here. Please, Sohne," Eohne's voice softened in her pleading. "He needs help. I can help him."

Sohne opened her eyes and looked at Eohne for the first time. "And what will you do? How will you help him? You don't even know where he is and you have no more data."

A rush of pleasure went through Eohne that she for once was a step ahead of the princess. "If Allan has been captured by the Gypsies and Willens of the Saour Desert, then one of two things will happen." Eohne stepped further into the space, capturing Sohne's eyes with her own. "They'll either eat him, or they'll sell him. Have you foreseen any of this?"

Sohne shook her head and stood, crossing her arms; the fabric of her gown floated across her body. "I have not seen anything about Jordan's father. It's strange, he is a void to me."

Eohne was disappointed, but would not let despair claim her yet. When Sohne had foresight about someone, she usually had foresight about that person's whole family, as though the premonitions came via genetics. *Perhaps the fact that Jordan is Arpak and Allan is human makes him inaccessible to Sohne.*

"He might be dead already," added Sohne, delivering the words gently.

"He might, but I refuse to accept that until I see a body. If he's been sold, then there is only one place within a hundred miles of that desert where the Gypsies can do that."

"Vischer," said Sohne, and Eohne nodded. Hope sprang up, lively and rich in Eohne's breast. *If Sohne were going to say no, she would have done so by now.*

Sohne went silent, her eyes down and her face thoughtful.

"The fungus is not in great danger, is it?" pressed Eohne. "I can resume my experiments when I return." If Eohne was honest with herself, she didn't believe the fungus could be synthesized with magic—but she was afraid of what Sohne would say if she admitted that out loud. *That's a problem for another day.*

Sohne nailed her with a look. "You need to fix those bugs, Eohne."

"I know," Eohne agreed, dropping her chin deferentially.

"Until you do, I don't think you should use them."

"Yes. Alright." At this point, Eohne would say whatever Sohne wanted to hear. The permission was so close she could taste it; her heart began to thump in eager anticipation. Once Sohne gave Eohne permission, the magic bonds that kept her tethered to the trees of Charra-Rae would fall away; Eohne would be free to act as she saw fit.

It was an intoxicating idea, that kind of freedom. Eohne had to admit that while saving Allan was her first priority, getting out of Charra-Rae for the first time since she was a young girl was an exhilarating bonus.

Maybe this is something I need in order to clear my own head. She'd been stuck in this forest, inventing and experimenting for years. Longing suddenly filled Eohne so swiftly and powerfully it was like a punch in the gut. Eohne's lips parted and she inhaled.

"You may go," said Sohne.

Eohne exhaled and her eyes shuttered closed. "Thank you, Sohne."

"You're welcome. But I have a condition."

"What's that?"

"You can't go alone. It's too dangerous."

Eohne's face expanded with surprise. *Sohne is giving me permission for not one, but* two *elves to leave Charra-Rae?*

"But who—"

"Not an Elf," said Sohne. "Pohle reported that a Nycht mercenary escorted Jordan here."

A name Jordan had mentioned in passing tugged at Eohne's memory. "Toth?"

"Is that his name? I'm told the two embraced before they parted. They are friends."

"But I don't know him. I don't even know what he looks like."

Sohne waved a hand. "Doesn't matter. You know where the Nychts of The Conca live."

"Yes, but—"

"I won't have one of my Elves venturing out of Charra-Rae on a dangerous rescue mission without help." She faced Eohne, stern in this directive. "Pohle said the Nycht was frightening. You convince him to accompany you, and you can go."

Eohne opened her mouth to protest, but she knew the look on Sohne's face. Resolve. There would be no changing her mind, and though Eohne bristled at the idea of taking the time to stop in The Conca, having a capable companion who knew Jordan could only be of benefit to them both.

"What if he refuses to come with me?"

"I don't think he will," mused Sohne. "But if he does, you need to return home so we can think of something else."

This was an unacceptable outcome. They didn't have time for that. Eohne was done dithering. *I have her permission, and once I am out of Charra-Rae, Sohne's powers can't force me to return. If the*

Nycht refuses, I will continue on alone. Eohne was grateful Sohne couldn't read her thoughts as she just nodded her agreement and turned for the door.

"Eohne?" Sohne's voice made the inventor pause and turn her ear to the princess.

"If he is alive, there is a good chance he'll have been taken on to Trevilsom. He won't have lingered in the cells of Vischer for long. The place has no resources; they won't want to keep him."

Eohne paused, taking this in. She hadn't considered what Allan's final destination would be if he made it as far as Vischer. "Trevilsom," she echoed.

"The island prison."

Eohne knew the place; there were few on Oriceran who didn't. It was the kind of place angry parents threatened their children with to get them to behave.

"That place has toxic magic," warned Sohne.

Eohne nodded. "I know." Once again, her fingertips had turned to ice. She clenched her jaw. "I'm not afraid."

"Fear is an exceptional motivator," responded the princess. "Maybe you should be."

Eohne faced Sohne, and gently bowed her head. "Good evening, Princess."

"Safe travels," Sohne replied.

Eohne left the princess's hut, bolting into a sprint as soon as the door closed behind her. A grin broke out on her face as she ran back to her lab. She charged through the door and began to gather things she would need for the journey: syringes, vials, her spinning cylinders and a number of other magical tools. Eohne strapped on her curved Elven blades, crisscrossing them over her upper back like two scythes. She stuffed a second set of clothes into her satchel, then grabbed enough food to get her beyond The Conca. She hurried out into the night and over the peaceful pathways of Charra-Rae, the sound of the waterfall growing louder.

CHAPTER 10

They came to take Marceau away first. Allan and Marceau spent their waking hours talking through the bars of their doors, seated on the cold hard floor. When Wilmot came to retrieve Marceau, the cheese importer cursed the guard up and down in French. The two prisoners were not allowed a moment to say goodbye and Marceau yelled out as he was escorted away.

"Je vais demander á tous que je connaisse," Marceau wheezed out desperately at his prison-mate. "Retarder le navire! Ne les laissez pas vous emmener!"

"Shut up," barked Wilmot, shaking Marceau and half dragging him down the hall.

Allan knew Marceau was speaking in French so the guard could not understand. Allan's own French was rusty, but he picked up the general message; delay the ship that would come to take Allan away.

Marceau's voice became muffled as the door at the end of the hall slammed shut. "Retarder le navire, mon ami!"

How was Allan supposed to delay the ship? Marceau had said he would ask everyone he knew for help. Allan felt hope fluttering in his chest. Could he dare expect a rescue? He had no idea how powerful Marceau's connections were, or if the Frenchman had any money or resources to pay for the help.

Allan stayed sitting by the door for a long time, feeling cold and bereft. Marceau was his only friend in this entire world aside from Jordan. He had learned so much from Marceau during their short time together. Allan mentally masticated all the things Marceau had shared as he waited for his 'blasted transport'.

"Oriceran is bigger than Earth," Marceau had said, his expressive eyes peering through the cell bars.

Allan wondered if he'd even recognize the man if he came across him down the road, for he'd come to know the Frenchman as a shadowed face, a set of eyes with pronounced purple bags under them, and a voice with a strong French accent.

"Many years ago there was a Great War," Allan was told. "But before that, many people from Earth had come to live here. That is why there are so many cultural similarity, so many language rooted in ours. After the War, portal travel became illegal. It still happen all the time," Marceau explained, his eyes full of compassion. "You just happen to be one who got caught. I think they are more concern with the appearance of upholding the law than actually upholding it. I have been using portals since I was a teenager. There is one not far from the grave of Karl Marx, in the Montmartre cemetery in Paris. Sometime I'm told they move, but mine has not moved, thank God. My father show it to me and pass me his business when he die." He crossed himself hurriedly and kissed his knuckle. "I still get afraid that my portal will not be there one day and I will become trapped on one side." He shuddered and became thoughtful. "Sometime I forget that most people on Earth still don't know about something that seem so normal to me."

"How do you travel back and forth so easily?"

"Oh, that is a very great secret," Marceau had replied with a hush in his voice. His eyes darted to the door at the end of the hall, fearful someone would overhear. "Even the walls can have ears, so be quiet and listen." His voice became a whisper. "If you need to travel, you only need two things."

Allan had leaned close to the bars, the cold metal pressing against the side of his face, his hand cupped behind his ear, straining to hear. "What's that?"

"Money or something of value to trade, and an Elf."

Allan stared at his prison-mate, his jaw slack. "An *Elf*, you say?" *I don't know why I'm so surprised—after all, I've seen talking rats already, and Marceau has talked of other magical species. Why not Elves?*

Marceau nodded solemnly. "If you have a chance to befriend one, or help one in need, you do so. They have the most powerful magic on Oriceran." He flapped a hand, "They are arrogant, but so are we French," he laughed. "So we are well suited."

Allan gave a half-smile. "I happen to like the French," he replied. Allan had spent a summer in the south of France learning how to make wine. He had learned a little of the language and a lot of the food. He was still sometimes nostalgic for that time; there was something simple about the French life that Allan missed. He had meant to take Jordan there before she started college, but the time seemed to slip away from him—now it was something he regretted not doing.

"Then you are God's own chosen," laughed Marceau. His laugh turned into a harsh cough. Allan frowned; he didn't like the sound of his friend's lungs.

"When did you last visit a doctor?" Allan asked when Marceau's coughing subsided.

"There is nothing a doctor can do for me, mon ami," Marceau replied matter-of-factly. "If I had stop smoking ten years ago, maybe," he shrugged.

The men had lapsed into silence, disappearing from their barred windows, but still sitting near their doors.

"Is there something an Elf could do?" Allan had asked, his eyes closed and his head leaning back against the cold wall.

"Sometime they try," came Marceau's voice. "They can help for a time—but the cough always return. We are not meant to live forever, so I do not mind. Death will fix me. Perhaps death will fix this broken heart of mine, also."

"Broken heart?" Allan's eyes opened. He knew all about broken hearts.

"Oui. Her name was Nannette."

Allan listened, and Marceau told of a French woman of great beauty. If Marceau was to be believed, Nannette could heal his every pain with a simple kiss and send the rain away with the wave of her hand. He had met her in Montmartre on the way to his portal with a load of cheese. He was punished by his father for being late with a shipment, but he did not care. Marceau was in love. He kept the portal a secret for a whole year while he and Nannette fell more deeply in love.

"I had to make an impossible choice," lamented Marceau, "between my father and my sweet Nannette. My father would not permit me to share our secret with anyone, but our business was good and it needed my attentions as my father got old. It was so difficult—soon impossible—to keep the portal and the business from Nannette." Marceau's voice grew thin. "So I shared it with her in the hopes that she would join me here."

"She wouldn't come to Oriceran?"

"She did!" Marceau exclaimed. "Mon ange was fearless. She was willing to leave her family for me."

"What happened?"

"I still cannot explain," croaked Marceau, and emotion threaded his words. "We pass through my portal together, using the relic the way I always did before. I pass through. Nannette did not. When I go back to retrieve her, she was not on the other side, either."

Allan let this sink in. "She just disappeared?" He lifted his head from the wall and peered through the bars at his friend, but Marceau was not visible.

"She was just gone; swallowed up in those horrible voices." The Frenchman's voice broke. "I will never forgive myself." These words were muffled, and Allan imagined Marceau's hands were covering his face. "After, I learned that my relic was not strong enough to let two pass. My father had never warned me this could happen, as he never expected me to break my promise."

"An Elf could not help to find Nannette?" Allan ventured, having no idea if what he suggested was ridiculous or not. It felt ridiculous to use the word 'Elf' in any serious conversation, but Marceau had said they were the most powerful beings here.

"Even the Elves I knew did not know how to bring her through. Some of them would not even let me speak of it." Marceau gave a heavy sigh.

"I'm so sorry, Marceau."

"Merci, mon ami. You can maybe see why I don't mind to die."

"But perhaps there is still a way?" Allan suggested. Like a slap in the face, his own words to Jordan came flying back to him at warp speed. He had admonished her for not letting go of her mother, and here he was encouraging Marceau to do the opposite.

"If there is, I do not know who to ask," replied Marceau flatly. "I have tried everything, everyone I could think of. Seems impossible."

They lapsed into stillness, listening to the endless breaking of the waves on the beach outside. Finally, Allan said, "I lost my love, too." What else was there in this cold, dank cell, but to commiserate with an understanding ear?

"What happened?" Marceau's voice became hushed and rapt.

Allan told Marceau of Jaclyn—how they'd met, how in love they'd been, of raising their family, of their travels and accomplishments. How, after Jordan had been born, Jaclyn had suffered from terrible post-partum depression, which clung to her like heavy, sodden drapes and showed no signs of lifting; then finally of Jaclyn's mysterious disappearance, and how Jordan had never given up hope.

"If this oak tree is a portal," wondered Marceau, "why could Jaclyn not be here?" He paused and added with a sour note, "If she did not get stuck in the in-between, like my Nannette."

This possibility broke over Allan like a polo mallet to the head, and a trembling hand flew to his mouth. *Marceau is right. Jaclyn could have fallen through the portal somehow, just the way Jordan did.* Allan squeezed his eyes shut and cursed himself for not thinking of it sooner. He put his fingertips to his temples; his brain was throbbing as a door opened that he had long since shut and thrown away the key for. He blew out a long, shuddering sigh. It was too much: the events of the last several weeks, the interdimnsional travel, landing here in this miserable place, the fate that awaited him and his helplessness to change it, and now the new possible explanation for Jaclyn's disappearance.

"Mon ami?" Marceau sounded worried.

"I'm here," Allan croaked. "You're right, of course. It never occurred to me before, but you are right. Jaclyn could be here, or —" he gulped, "in the in-between."

"Mmmmm," Marceau rumbled a comforting, sympathetic sound. "Now I am the sorry one for you." He sighed. "Seems we are both in a bad way."

"I think I am in a worse way than you," Allan opined. "Seems you have a way out; you are just waiting for a letter, right?"

"Oui."

"I am headed to a place called 'Trevilsom.'"

"Oh, merde." The sound of movement from Marceau's cell made Allan look through the bars. Marceau's eyes appeared, wide and frightened. "You cannot go there, mon ami!"

Allan gave a humorless laugh. "Do you have any suggestions on how I can change my fate? I have no magic, like these Elves you speak of."

Marceau's eyes darted around; his mind was racing. His fingers wrapped around the bars, unfeeling of the cold.

That was when the door at the end of the hall had banged open, and Wilmot came to retrieve Marceau.

Later that afternoon, Allan's transport came. He was unceremoniously removed from his cell and taken out of the prison and down to the beach, where a ship was waiting to receive him.

CHAPTER 11

Opening their wings to catch the air like parachutes, Jordan and Sol drifted down into a labyrinth of walkways and shops in a slow, lazy spiral. They returned to Middle Rodania first thing in the morning, right after breakfast. Belshar's office was only three levels below Juer's library. They landed with a hop and a skip on a wooden platform.

The street was bustling and full of action, and Jordan found it difficult to keep up with Sol as she gaped at the shop windows and the curiously dressed, non-Strix species having animated conversations in the middle of the street. Blue received more than his share of curious glances, but everyone seemed so preoccupied that they would simply stare, jaws slack, before tearing their eyes away to barrel onward.

Sol stopped outside of a squat wooden tower that looked like it had too many doors. People bustled continuously in and out while bells rang and chatter filled the air.

"You don't need to come in with me," Sol said, eyeing the frenetic pace around the building. "It'll be faster if I just zip in and out. If you want, just hang out and look around. I'll be as quick as I can."

"Okay," Jordan flashed him a smile. "There are a lot of interesting shops back there."

Sol nodded. "Don't go too far?"

"I won't. You're my bread and butter, remember?"

"Right." Sol turned and entered the shop behind a tall skinny Nycht carrying an armload of scrolls.

"What are you grinning about?" a wingless lady barked at him from behind the front desk. Her hair was frazzled in a red cloud around her wide face and her glasses were askew. A thin sheen of sweat coated her forehead. A long line of bell pulls lined the wall behind her, each with a name engraved below it; 'Belshar Zak' was one of those names. It took Sol a moment to realize the woman was talking to him.

"Oh, nothing." *Was I grinning?* He wiped the smile off his face. "I'm looking for Belshar."

"Ha!" Her not-inconsiderable chest bounced. "Everyone's looking for Belshar," she croaked, and Sol had the vague impression of a smug toad on a lilypad.

"It's important," Sol said.

"Oh, it's *important,* is it?" She followed this with a wheezing laugh. She set meaty fists on her broad hips. "Do you have an appointment, Mr. 'It's Important'?"

"No, but—" Sol reached for his satchel.

"Shoo, then! Handsome as a devil and presumptuous as a lawyer, this one." She grumbled to herself as she flapped one hand at him and passed the other over her forehead. She yanked a book toward her on the desk and slammed it open. "Come back in…" She trailed a finger down the page. "Three weeks."

Sol held a ring out for her to see: a thick, gold band crested the king's seal.

The fat lady frowned and shoved her glasses up her nose. She looked down at the ring, then up at Sol's face, then down at the ring again. " 'Zat real?"

"Of course," Sol answered patiently.

"Why ain't you wearing it?" Her face was progressively growing pinker.

"It makes people act funny when they see it," Sol said. *Kind of like how you're acting now that you've seen it.* He slipped it over the knuckle of the fourth finger of his right hand to show her it fit him perfectly. The king's signets were magic; if anyone who hadn't officially been given the seal tried to don one, they'd lose a finger.

She gave an uncomfortable laugh out of one side of her mouth. "Bet it does." She jerked her chin at the narrow stairway to her left, and her chins wobbled to show they also agreed. "Belshar is on the fifth floor."

"Thank you," Sol gave her a dazzling smile. "Will you ring his bell and let him know I'm coming, please? The name is Solomon Donda."

She nodded and shooed him up the stairs. He turned sideways to shuffle up the tight stairs and heard her mutter, "You can ring *my* bell, anytime," under her breath. Then louder and into the voicebox Sol knew would deliver right to Belshar's office, "Solomon Donda. King's seal on him."

Sol had to squeeze by three others before reaching the fifth floor. There were several polite head nods, and *'excuse me's* in two different languages. Belshar's was the only office on the fifth floor. Sol had never met the bureaucrat, but he'd been mentioned in passing. Belshar was trademaster for Middle Rodania and Lower Rodania—a desk-job Sol would rather die than have.

Belshar's office door was closed, so Sol waited just outside. He peered through the warped glass window looking down into the street, wondering what fun shop Jordan was exploring and wishing he was with her instead.

The door opened with a rusty scream and a squat, wingless man waddled out with a sheaf of papers under his arms and a harassed look on his face. Ignoring Sol, he waddled down the stairs, bumping against the wall like he'd been drinking since noon.

"Donda?" A thin reedy voice called from the office.

Sol poked his head in. The magnitude of disaster that greeted him temporarily froze Sol's tongue in his mouth. Piles of papers, envelopes, books, scrolls and other busywork towered haphazardly from every surface. A wooden installation with at least fifty boxes was stuffed with multi-colored papers and rolls. The room was furry with dust that was never fully given a chance to settle, as the small Nycht behind the desk frantically shuffled, stacked, stamped, folded, and signed one thing after another.

Belshar had a narrow, pale countenance, wore glasses that were far too large for his face, and had long, dark hair threaded with gray that was tied back. A few wiry strands refused to be tamed and stuck up from his temples in frazzled coils. His high forehead glowed with sweat and dark circles ringed his eyes. He fixed Sol with the glare of the overworked, which was laced with fear that whoever walked through his door came with more work attached.

"You're from the king?" he asked, speaking quickly and with no small amount of dread. "I'm a very busy Nycht."

"I can see that," replied Sol. He held his signet up where Belshar could see it. "I come on behalf of Juer."

Belshar frowned. "The Royal Doctor? What could he possibly want with me?"

"You're in charge of trade agreements with Maticaw?" Sol entered the small room and tightened his wings behind him so he didn't knock anything over.

Belshar bobbed his head impatiently. "Maticaw, Skillen, Operyn." Belshar named the three major port cities nearest Rodania. "Any one of them would be a full-time job." He shuffled through the papers in his hand and seemed to find what he was looking for. Taking the page out, he laid it flat on his desk and put the rest aside. "What of it?"

"There is a medicine that Rodania imports from Maticaw, usually through Cles, the Apothecary."

Belshar peered over the tops of his glasses at Sol; his green eyes locked on the Arpak's face and widened. It seemed this might be a topic that was worthy of his attention. "What medicine?"

"It's called lapita."

Belshar blinked, thinking. "I don't know this 'lapita'." He put a hand out. "Wait." He spun in his chair to face the back of the room and scanned the wall of endless documents. "Lapita, lapita…"

"I'm not sure the problem lies with the medicine itself—" Sol began.

Belshar snapped a hand into the air, requesting silence. Sol closed his mouth with a smile and waited. Bureaucrats like Belshar were considered below couriers like Sol, but more often than not, they acted as though it were the other way around.

Several minutes walked by as the Nycht searched the wall. He pulled out documents, flipped through them, opened and scanned scrolls. Sol crossed his arms and his foot tapped absently. He wondered how well the Nycht might receive the concept of alphabetization.

Finally, Belshar spun back to the Arpak with a tattered, single page in his hand. "There is no problem with the trade of lapita. It can be purchased in any amount and shipped into Rodania without delay."

"The main ingredient in lapita is gersher fungus," Sol replied patiently.

Belshar's face fell visibly.

"I see you know what gersher fungus is."

"Yes," the Nycht admitted. "Yes, I do." He heaved a sigh and took his glasses off, rubbing at the red marks on the bridge of his nose.

"You're aware of a problem, then?"

"It's this new portmaster in Maticaw," Belshar burst out dramatically. "Jack something-or-other." He tossed his glasses onto his desk with something like disgust. "A more disagreeable trade partner I have never had to suffer before. It's like he actually enjoys tangling up progress in mountains of paperwork and layers of bureaucracy."

"He's stalling the import of the fungus with paperwork?"

"Yes!" Belshar paused. "No." He picked his glasses up and put them back on. "To be honest, I haven't had time to find out why he's stalling the import yet. I have—" he gestured helplessly to the mountains of documents on his desk. "This."

"The royal doctor is asking you to make it a priority," replied Sol. "I'm sorry you have so much work, but that medicine is very likely meant for a member of the royal family, or for one of the council members. Can you not hire an assistant?"

"There is no budget for that," said Belshar in a tone that said the topic had been broached many times and dismissed just as many times.

"There might be a very simple reason for the delay," ventured Sol. "Perhaps it could be solved in a matter of minutes if you were to go to Maticaw and see him in person…?"

"These things are never simple," argued Belshar. "And I don't have time to fly all the way to Maticaw for a single item of dispute. I have over two thousand disputes right here that I have to deal with."

"Send someone else, then." Sol was rapidly losing patience.

"There is no one else. I told you," Belshar snapped. "You don't understand. If I take time away from this desk, all things get delayed. Something has to give. If it's not the gersher fungus, it's the cheese from Usenno, or the oyo feathers from Operyn, or the butter diamonds from Skillen."

"Who makes the decision about what gets priority? You?"

"Me?" Belshar gave a bitter laugh. "I wish. It's the squeaky wheel that—" he paused as Sol stepped forward.

Sol planted a closed fist on Belshar's desk and leaned toward the Nycht. Belshar leaned back in tandem, his jaw going slack and his eyes widening. Sol held up his hand, where the royal signet glittered in the dull light from the single cobwebby window. Sol's wings snapped open with a dull pop and the tips of his feathers mashed against the wall. The wind he created blew the papers off Belshar's desk.

"The 'squeaky wheel,' you say?" Sol narrowed his eyes into a glare. He made another fist and thumped it on the desk. "Squeak."

CHAPTER 12

Jordan wandered the streets of Middle Rodania with Blue in her arms. The smells of fresh-baked goods, spices, and flowers mingled with other, less pleasant smells like oil, burnt metal, and smoke. The shops were narrow and tall, with wide doors to accommodate Rodania's winged citizens. Some shops were outdoors with only a tent over their goods. Rodania's citizens and visitors bustled and bartered, ambled and chatted.

It's not so different from shopping in downtown Richmond, thought Jordan. An upset looking man no taller than Jordan's knee, with purple skin and carrying a huge dead beetle, rushed by as though taking the beetle to emergency care. *The people are a little more curious,* she thought as she stepped aside to allow him passage.

Blue gave a squeak, jumped out of her arms and wove his way through the legs of passing shoppers.

"Blue, where are you going?"

The dragon waddled under a tent covering tables full of strange contraptions, found a bench against a wall, and crawled into the shadow underneath it. He curled up like an overheated dog in the shade and blew out a breath, sending a cloud of dust across Jordan's boots as she bent over to look at him. "You want to sleep? We only got up a couple hours ago." Blue turned his head to the side and closed his eyes. "Fine, but what if someone decides they'd like a pet dragon and snatches you up?"

Blue blinked and lifted his head. He gave three sharp snaps in the air, displaying razor-sharp teeth, and then laid his chin on his front claws again.

"Right. You'll take their fingers off. Got it." Jordan got to her feet feeling unsure as to whether she should leave Blue there alone or not. She frowned. *I can't be with him every single minute of his life; I'll have to learn to trust him sooner or later.*

She turned away and her eye caught on something familiar—something from home. Her eyes widened as she walked up to the antique gramophone. It was similar to the one the Kacys had in their parlor back home; beautiful, with a copper horn and crank, and glossy wooden bracket. The turntable glittered with what looked like black granite and she bent for a closer look. There was an embossed stamp, a glyph of some kind, pressed into the end of the copper crank. Jordan ran her finger over it.

"Isn't it charming?"

Jordan jumped and turned to see a Nycht emerging from the shop, wiping her hands on a dirty towel. She was very petite; the top of her head barely reached Jordan's shoulder. Her wings were a rich chocolate brown, her skin only a few shades lighter. Coal black eyes glittered at the gramophone with affection. Her hair was knotted into dreadlocks and tied up on top of her head like a thick bouquet, the ends spraying up and out in all directions. Gold jewelry sparkled in her ears. Her face was angular and lit with fierce intelligence.

"Where did you get this?" Jordan asked. She was about to add that her family had one similar to it, but thought that might lead in the direction of portals.

"I reverse engineered it from a sample brought over from Earth," replied the Nycht. "I'm Arth."

"Jordan." She smiled at the Nycht. "You made this?"

Jordan wasn't sure what surprised her more—the fact that the Nycht had made a perfect copy of a gramophone, or that she had mentioned Earth so casually.

"I made everything," said Arth, gesturing wide at the array of complicated looking items scattered about in front of her shop. "It's what I do. That's my stamp on the crank there; it's my last name in Rodanian."

"A single glyph?" Jordan peered at the mark. Looking closer, she saw it wasn't a single glyph, but a number of short curves and lines that, from far away, looked connected.

"You don't speak Rodanian?" Arth arched an eyebrow and glanced at Jordan's wings.

"Uh, not…very well," Jordan stuttered. "Does it work?"

"Of course it works!" Arth looked affronted.

"I mean, do you have records to play on it?"

"Oh." Her face fell. "I don't, no. Those are difficult to come by." Arth brightened momentarily "Not impossible, though, if you know the right people." Her face froze for a second, and then she blinked up at Jordan, realizing she might have said something compromising. She put her hands up. "Not me, though. I don't do that kind of thing."

"Your work is remarkable," complimented Jordan. "This is for sale, right?"

Arth nodded vigorously. "Everything is."

"Forgive me, but what is the point of purchasing a gramophone when there are no records to play on it?"

"Really?" Arth looked surprised. "Most of my customers are not looking to use the things they purchase from me. They are collectors." She stroked the bell of the gramophone. "The fact that it is a replica of something taken from Earth is enough of a selling feature." She cocked a dark eyebrow at Jordan. "You're not from here, are you?"

"No."

"Where are you from?"

"Oh, beyond," replied Jordan vaguely. "Do you have anything else that you've reverse engineered from Earth?"

Arth brightened again. "Lots of things! Come in." She turned and disappeared through the doorway of her workshop.

With a last glance at the sleeping dragon under the bench, Jordan followed her.

The shop smelled of rubber and wood, grease and burnt metal. Tables and floor space at the front of the shop were cluttered with complicated looking items. Most of them were not familiar to Jordan, until she spied a grandfather clock.

"Wow!" She took in the clock that towered over them, its face an elaborate display of flourishes and semi-precious stones.

"You like this one?" Arth stopped so Jordan could admire it. "The original was made with tortoiseshell," explained Arth, her eyes skimming the elegant curves of the clock's face. "But I don't use animal parts in anything I make." She shuddered. "I'm not sure why they do that on Earth; humans are so barbaric."

"I suppose," replied Jordan weakly.

Beside the grandfather clock sat an old radio of the type produced in the '60s. Next to that lay a large hand-bellows, and an old-fashioned typewriter. An antique rifle stood against the wall in the corner, its barrel pointing to the sky. Jordan couldn't tell how old the rifle that it had been modelled after would have been. *Allan would know*, she thought with a pang.

"Did you make that, too?" Jordan pointed to the rifle.

"Of course. I made everything."

"Does it work?"

"In theory. I believe it requires something that we do not manufacture in Rodania." Arth closed her eyes, thinking hard. "Some kind of powder…"

"Gunpowder?" supplied Jordan.

Arth's eyes popped open. "Yes! How did you know that?"

Jordan shrugged. "Fount of useless knowledge," she smiled.

"Where did you say you were from?" Arth's eyes narrowed and seemed to trace Jordan's features with more scrutiny than before.

"Oh, down a ways…" Jordan began to wilt under the Nycht's probing gaze. "I really should be getting on." She turned toward the door. "Remarkable work you do here."

"Wait—" Arth followed her.

"Someone is expecting me. Delightful to have met you." She left the shop and bent to look under the bench. "Blue. Time to go."

The dragon yawned and got up. He stretched and gave a squeak of dislike at being woken.

"How do you know so much about Earth?" Arth asked, following Jordan out into the street.

"I've read a lot," Jordan skirted. "Now, Blue." Her tone was sharp as she called him again. Blue made a flapping leap into Jordan's arms, and she grunted as the reptile hit her stomach. She looked down at him in surprise. *Does he seem bigger than yesterday?*

"You have a dragon?" Arth gaped at the reptile in Jordan's arms.

"He sort of adopted me. Lovely to meet you," Jordan shot the Nycht a big smile and wandered down the street before she could be asked anything else. She could feel Arth's eyes on her back as she strolled away.

* * *

Heading in the direction of Belshar's office, Jordan took a bridge across the gap to the other side. Blue perked up, stretching his neck. He squawked and bounced out of her arms, his claws clicking across the stones as he disappeared between people's legs and down a dark alley.

"Blue?" Jordan peered into the narrow space. It wasn't wide enough for her to squeeze through with her wings.

"Did he imprint on you?" came a raspy voice from an open shop door.

Jordan looked over to see a small wizened and wingless man cleaning a set of paintbrushes with a wet rag. His seamed face was open and his blue eyes warm. His complexion was rosy, including the tip of his nose.

"Yes. You know about dragon imprinting?"

"There's only three known species that do it," the man replied, inspecting the fibers of the brushes in his hands. He blew on them and nodded with approval. "He must have imprinted on you, otherwise he wouldn't be here. Yes?"

"Yes."

"Then don't worry about him. When he's finished his little adventure, he'll find you." The old man turned and shuffled inside his shop.

Jordan peered through the door and followed the man inside, where she saw that the place was stuffed to the gills with artwork. "Did you do all of these?"

"Many of them, but not all," the man's voice drifted out from behind a large canvas propped on an easel. His face appeared beside it. "Like art, do you?"

A large window overhead allowed natural light to stream down on the man and his canvas.

"Some of it," Jordan said. "I was a fan of Mucha when I was growing up."

"Who?"

Jordan flushed. "No one special."

She stopped in front of a miniature portrait of a man in a strange uniform. She narrowed her eyes at the artwork. *What is it that seems so familiar?* It certainly wasn't the subject—he had green hair and was wearing a bright yellow double-breasted jacket with a solid red stripe down the side.

Jordan gasped.

The style! The same soft application of color, the way the light plays across the man's cheekbones and brows. She yanked the locket out from under her vest and popped it open. She held the locket up beside the portrait, her skin marbling with gooseflesh.

"Is this your work?" Jordan breathed, her heart pounding and crawling up her throat with the realization that the artists had to be one and the same.

There was a thud as the man hopped down from a stool, and he appeared in the narrow aisle where Jordan stood in front of the painting.

"Lovely work, isn't it?" The old man patted his chest absently. "It's not mine; this was done by a fellow named Five Hurley. What have you got there?" He peered at the open locket.

"The style looks the same, don't you think?" Jordan held the locket up so he could see it and compare the two portraits.

"That it does," he confirmed.

Jordan's face lit up and her heart pounded with a rush of hope. "Does this artist live here, on Middle Rodania? I need to meet him. This portrait is of my mother; she disappeared when I was a little girl and I've been looking for her."

The man's face fell. "Oh, I am sorry. Five died a few years ago, now. His work fetches a pretty price, I can tell you that."

Jordan's heart plummeted.

The man's bushy brows shot up. "But you might have everything you need right here, my dear!"

"What do you mean?"

"Five was a Light Elf. A lot of his work was done with magic paint."

"Magic paint?"

"The paint was imbued with power as it was applied. It acts as a compass of sorts, leading the way to whose countenance the art portrays."

Jordan took a breath. She stared at the portrait in wonder. Jaclyn's beautiful face stared back at her, calm and serene, as if to say *'I knew you'd discover my secret. So what are you waiting for?'*

"A compass," Jordan whispered, holding the locket in her hand. "How does it work?"

"From what I know," the man disclosed, "the magic could be purchased in varying degrees of power; the stronger the magic, the more expensive the work. When the paint comes within a predetermined radius of the subject, the paint will be drawn home, so to speak."

Jordan smacked her forehead with her palm as a memory came rushing back to her: the locket floating up in front of her face the day she'd met Blue.

"She's in Maticaw! Oh!" She danced on her toes, almost unable to comprehend the meaning as it barrelled into her all at once. "The locket, it drifted up."

"Drifted up?" echoed the elderly man. "That is certainly a good sign. Yes."

"It floated up from my neck, it was the weirdest—" Jordan panted with excitement. "I thought it was just one of those crazy Oriceran things."

The old man chuckled and crossed his arms. "Not much experience with magic, eh? Most Strix don't. So, you have your answer."

Jordan squeaked with joy. She grinned at the man, her eyes shining. Unable to contain herself, she threw her arms around him.

"Thank you, thank you! You have no idea how much this means. Thank you!"

The man started then laughed. He patted her arm. "You're welcome."

Jordan released him and headed for the door, then turned back as another thought struck her. "Do you know who would have commissioned this? It wouldn't have been my mother, would it? That wouldn't make sense; why would you have a compass made that points to yourself?"

"No, it wouldn't likely have been her. Unless it was given as a gift?"

"Right." Jordan chewed her lip, absorbing this new idea. Another mystery unfolded in her brain, like a flower missing several petals. "Thank you again. Goodbye!"

"Good bye, my dear." The old man watched the yellow-winged Arpak disappear from his shop. "Good luck."

CHAPTER 13

*E*ohne watched from behind a cluster of boulders as three harpies screamed and warbled on The Conca floor up ahead. Their scabby bald heads bobbed down out of view as they ripped and tore at their meal, then bobbed up again to look around, their beaks dripping with black blood and pieces of rotten meat. At least Eohne was downwind so they couldn't smell her crouching among the dusty rocks less than five hundred paces away. The downside of being downwind was the putrid smell. She put a hand over her nose and breathed through her mouth. There was no time to wait for the overgrown buzzards to finish their meal and move on.

Eohne reached into her satchel and pulled out a stone cylinder, which had a second cylinder made of alabaster inserted inside. She reached behind her head and grabbed one of her curved blades. She could do a lot with her kind of magic, but it always seemed to require some kind of bodily fluid to work. *One day, I will figure out how to tap into a being's frequency without asking for blood or spittle or urine. Until then...*

Pricking her finger with the blade's tip, she squeezed a drop of blood into the reservoir in the center of the cylinder. She sucked on her thumb and held the cylinder out in front of her, parallel with her hips. The inner cylinder began to spin inside the outer, making a soft whirring sound. A light began to grow inside, sending rays straight out the ends, which then curved up and down and around Eohne's frame until the rays met above and below her, making a bubble around her. The light and sound faded, but the protective field remained. Eohne held the cylinder steadily in front of her hips and resumed walking. The sounds of her footsteps and her breathing echoed around her inside the small space. Sound waves couldn't get out, but they could certainly come in, and so could the air. Eohne could smell the harpies and hear them warbling and tearing at flesh and bone.

She walked past the three black beasts and paused to take a closer look. They were each well over twelve feet tall, but one of them—the one with the wide, curving horns—must have been close to sixteen or seventeen feet. One of the smaller ones had the two short horns protruding from her knobby skull—a promise of larger horns to come. They curved down toward her beak, giving off an ugly, demonic impression. Eohne avoided looking at the carcass they were dining on, but from the corner of her eye, she caught a single great, curved horn thrusting upward from a mess of black feathers.

They are eating their own kind. Eohne had a strong stomach, but with this realization, she swallowed down a heave and moved swiftly on.

Several minutes later, when the three harpies were well behind her, Eohne spotted a large curved thing in the dirt and she paused to look down at it. It was the other horn, broken off the dead harpy's skull as though sliced through cleanly with a blade. Eohne continued on, but paused again when she came to the scuff marks and black pools of dried blood in the middle of The Conca's gorge. When she started moving again, she increased her pace, still holding the cylinder steadily in front of her hips.

As night was falling, Eohne took a break to eat and rest. Crawling into a low cave in the gorge wall, she pulled out a bag of mixed nuts and berries and munched on them as she considered the cool shadow creeping up the far side of the gorge wall as the sun set. She took long draughts of water from her water horn and when she was satisfied, put away the food and drink and rummaged in her bag for something else.

She pulled out a small round disk of glass and a string of vials all linked together. Eohne set the disk on the dirt in between her long legs, which were stretched straight out in front of her. She held the vials up to what little light she had and read the labels of each one silently until she found the one marked 'Nycht'. She unhinged the vial from the rest and removed the tiny stopper. Upturning the vial, she held her breath as a single drop of the fluid rolled out and splashed onto the surface of the disk. Careful not to use any more of the precious fluid, she stoppered it and put it back into its place in the links. It wasn't as good as blood, since it was generic Nycht frequency made from soaking a strand of Nycht hair in a leeching concoction she'd made, but it would do the trick.

Eohne picked up the disk and rolled it in her hand so that the fluid spread out evenly over the depression in the glass, covering it from edge to edge. The fluid then congealed with a *snap*, and rolled back together into a single drop. The drop turned a bright, illuminated orange and sat in the top right corner of the disk. No matter which way Eohne turned the disk, even if she tilted it right on its side or spun it with her fingers, that orange light would lead the way. Putting the rest of her things away, Eohne left the cave and began to walk on in the dark. The evening was cool, but the air was still. Conca insects chirruped, keeping Eohne company. The sky became a strip of stars overhead, a long spectacular ribbon of twinkling lights and galaxies.

When she grew tired, she swallowed a bean not unlike the one she'd given Jordan, only this one would give her a kind of twilight consciousness—allowing her to get the restful benefits of sleep without having to stop and make camp.

As the sun was beginning to make whispers of light in the strip of sky overhead, Eohne's twilight consciousness wore off, and she blinked awake. Looking down at the disk in her hand, she noted that the orange light had shifted to the three o'clock position. Eohne looked up and saw a tall, dark crack in the gorge wall just up ahead.

She squeezed into the narrow passage, noting that the gorge opened wide again up ahead, creating a whole second alleyway that branched off the main Conca. The orange light shifted again on its glass surface, and its message was clear: *dead ahead*.

As the sun rose, the gorge revealed itself to be very broad, and the walls were not quite as high as those she had passed through previously. Dark recesses and caves speckled both sides ahead and the sounds of a waterfall reached her ears. Another seam opened to the right where she could see a sparkling pool of bubbling water; the morning sun had already found it and turned it bright aqua. Greenery sprang up around the banks of the pool, and Eohne thought she saw the shape of something dart past.

A Nycht, taking a morning bath?

But the disk told her to press forward, so she did. The orange dot did not show the location of any one particular Nycht, but rather the direction in which the biggest number of them lay. Eohne had no idea how many Nychts lived in this gorge, but she told herself that she had no reason to fear them; Nychts and Elves had no squabbles that she knew of. Still, she was walking straight into the heart of their home, she wasn't sure they would appreciate being found so easily.

The cool feeling of being watched trailed its fingers across Eohne's neck and she resisted the urge to use the cylinder to hide herself.

When two Nychts dropped out of the sky in front of her, landing on the dusty floor of the canyon like two boulders hewn from the rock above, Eohne didn't even jump. She just stopped walking and put the glass disk into her bag, keeping her eyes on the visitors as she did so.

"Hello," she greeted the pair softly. "I'm happy to have found you."

The two Nychts shared a look. The man was huge and barrel-chested, with a round belly to match, while the woman was lean as a whip. Both of them were armed. Hilts glittered from leather holsters, loops of rope hung from hips, spikes protruded from leather armor, and the woman had no small amount of piercings to augment the overall menacing impression.

"You think you're just going to walk into Noriloth like you own the place?" the woman hissed in a strange accent, then spat off to the side and crossed her sinewy arms. Her pitch-black bat's wings shuddered and tightened, the hooked claws curling in on themselves the way a fist might clench. The woman was deeply tanned, and her unfriendly eyes were as green as moss. Her teeth were perfect and so white they were almost painful to look at, but Eohne didn't miss the slightly-too-long eye teeth; she wondered if they were filed to look that way, or if the woman had been born with them.

"Of course not," Eohne dropped her chin. "This is your home, I regret that I had to come in unannounced. I am looking for someone."

The woman gave a short, nasty laugh, but the big man put out a hand and silenced her. It was clear which of the two was in charge.

The big male Nycht had light gray wings and one of his claws was broken. He was wrapped in the black leather vest of his kind, all his skin protected, save for his thick beefy arms, which were as pale as a moon and dusted with freckles. His hair was short and covered his skull like red grass. His vivid blue eyes had a kindness that was lacking in the woman's.

"I can help you with that," said Eohne, gesturing to the broken dewclaw.

The Nycht glanced up at the broken claw and then back at her, an eyebrow raised. "It'll grow back," he said gruffly.

"Yes, but I can make it grow back now. It won't even hurt; it's just a nail. You can't climb because of it, right?" Eohne had a hard time picturing a man of his size climbing anything at all, regardless of how many dewclaws he had, but Strix had hollow bones and could be much more nimble than they looked.

"We don't need anything from you," the woman barked.

Again the man put his hand out, and Eohne caught a fleeting expression of tried patience.

"What do you want?" the man said. "We don't see Elves in these parts. I'm curious."

"I need to find one of your brothers," said Eohne. "His name is Toth."

The man's face expanded with surprise, and the woman darted a sideways look at him, her eyes wide.

The man grunted. "How did you know he's my brother?"

It was Eohne's turn to be surprised. She gave a laugh. "I used 'brother' in the figurative sense; I didn't realize you were actually related to him."

"What do you want with him?"

"One of our mutual friends is in trouble," explained Eohne. "I've come to let him know and ask for his help."

"He won't help you," sneered the woman. "There isn't nobody who could be his friend *and* your friend. Nychts don't have friends outside our own—"

"Chayla," said the man with a weary sideways glance. "Enough."

The woman glared at her companion, then wilted under his gaze. She shot a resentful look at Eohne but shut her mouth.

"Who is in trouble?"

"A girl named Jordan whom he recently escorted into Charra-Rae. I think—" Eohne shifted uncomfortably and hoped she didn't misspeak. "If you'll take me to him, he can at least decide if he wants to help her." Eohne watched the man's face, his expression said that Jordan's name was not entirely foreign to him. She felt safe enough to introduce herself. "My name is Eohne."

"Caje," said the Nycht without hesitating. He relaxed his arms. "You have a deal. You fix my dewclaw, and I'll take you to Toth."

Chayla's mouth gaped, but Caje turned to her and said, "Go. Let him know we're coming."

Chayla frowned, but she'd been given an order. She turned and flapped into the air, disappearing down the gorge.

"Thank you," said Eohne, relieved. She rummaged in her bag and retrieved the glass disk. Then she wiped away the orange dot, as it had done its job.

"Now if you'll just spit on this, please."

* * *

TOTH WADED out of the crystalline pool where fresh, cold water bubbled up from underground. Naked and shivering, Toth reached for the fabric that would serve as his towel—it had probably once been a bed sheet for some farmer in The Conca.

He scrubbed at his wet hair with the sheet and flapped his wings, sending spray in all directions. Nychts didn't wash their wings unless they knew they were safe, since water hampered their ability to fly. It was still possible to fly, but it was laborious and left them exposed.

When Toth had stripped off and walked into the pool, his duty was done for the day, and he was alone. Or so he'd thought.

"You might want to put pants on."

Toth scrambled to get the bed sheet off his face. "Chayla," he barked. "What are you doing here?" Water dripped into his eyes from his hair and ran down his muscular frame in rivulets. His silver hair spiked out in all directions like needles. Chayla had snuck up on him more than once since she'd joined the rebels two years ago and he cursed her under his breath for it. No one was as silent as Chayla. It wasn't so much the catching him naked as it was that she made him feel like he was losing his edge, getting old.

Chayla was crouched on a rock with her knees tucked up to her chest, her wings relaxed and trailing in the dust behind her. She grinned her blazing white toothy grin and didn't look away from Toth's nakedness. "There is someone here to see you."

"Besides you?" Toth grumbled, wiping droplets from his belly and chest. He turned his back to Chayla and draped the makeshift towel over his hips so it hung down to his knees. It was enough to cover his butt while he pulled on his leather pants—a job in itself, over damp skin.

Chayla frowned and cocked her head sideways, trying to peer under the hem of Toth's bed sheet. "Prude."

Caje appeared in the fissure between the rocks just beyond Chayla; someone else Toth couldn't see was following behind him.

"Can't even take a bath around here..." Toth muttered. He did up the buckle of his belt and watched his brother approach.

Toth's gaze fell on the Elf as she stepped around the huge Nycht. She was tall and willowy with long, wavy brunette hair and dark eyes. She carried several bags crisscrossed over her body, and her clothing was simple: a tunic over loose pants, cinched by a three-buckled leather belt. The hilts of two curved blades, typical of the Elves of Charra-Rae, were strapped across her back in easy reaching distance and visible just above her shoulders. Elves were known for their ability to draw a blade and make a cut in the same motion, usually resulting in a lost limb or a lost head. *Interesting that Caje didn't ask this Elf to remove her weapons; it's a sign he has some level of trust in her.*

His eyes flicked to Caje's wings. His brother's broken dewclaw was now whole and as black and shiny and sharp as ever. *Only Elf magic could have done that, and there is only one Elf in the vicinity.* Toth found himself full of curiosity.

"You're Toth?" The Elf stepped forward. "I'm Eohne."

Toth felt a vibration twang through his middle as she spoke, that string running the length of his spine that only Charra-Rae Elves had the ability to pluck.

"I apologize for the poor timing," Eohne said, her eyes tracing the scars crisscrossing Toth's bare chest and arms. "Didn't realize you were bathing."

"Not your fault," replied Toth, shooting a glare at his brother while he pulled his vest on, reaching back to yank on the laces below his wings. "Chayla?" His eyes flashed to the Nycht still crouched on the rock and observing the whole exchange with interest. He jerked his head toward the fissure. *Beat it.*

Chayla rolled her eyes and moved extra slow. She dragged herself to standing and sauntered back the way she'd come, keeping an ear cocked in their direction until she disappeared into the fissure.

"What I've come to tell you has to do with Jordan," Eohne said. Her dark eyes flashed to Caje momentarily.

Toth finished putting himself back together by strapping his throwing blades on, and came to stand before Eohne.

"Would you like to sit? I can't offer you much more hospitality than that, I'm afraid. We're unaccustomed to guests here in Noriloth. But please," he gestured to the cluster of flat stones near the pool.

Eohne took a seat on one of the rocks. "I wasn't sure who else to go to with this information and Jordan told me how kind you were to her."

"What information?" Toth stayed standing, and Caje stood behind him, listening with his arms crossed over his chest.

Eohne eyed Toth, uncertain of her footing here. The Nychts

were polite but cool, and the mention of Jordan's name hadn't thawed Toth any. "You're friends with Jordan, right? She gave that impression."

"Nychts don't have friendships with humans," Toth said.

"She's not human," countered Eohne.

Toth blinked. "Excuse me?"

"She's Strix."

Eohne could see thunderheads forming in Toth's expression; probably at what he perceived to be some kind of deception on Jordan's part.

"Is this a joke?" Toth looked at his brother, who only shrugged and made a face that said, *'Don't look to me for answers. I've no idea what's going on here.'*

"No, it's not a joke." Eohne answered him. "She didn't know she was Strix, either, or I'm sure she would have told you. Jordan is from Earth."

Toth's eyes widened and he belted out an unexpected laugh. Eohne and Caje both stared at him. "That explains a few things."

Eohne smiled. "It does, doesn't it?" Even if she hadn't had an accent, Jordan's naiveté and her wonder at everything surrounding her was a dead giveaway of her mundane upbringing. Eohne guessed that Toth had seen his share of this behavior from the Earthling, too.

Toth's laughter faded, but his smile remained. "What's that got to do with me?"

"Hear me out." Eohne, uncomfortable with being the only one sitting, got to her feet. "I'm an inventor. I'm good at what I do, but my magic isn't perfect. No magic is." Eohne began to use her hands to talk; it helped her get through the story under Toth's penetrating gaze. "I invented these messenger bugs. I know that's a terrible name, very boring, but I haven't had time to name them properly yet."

Toth and Caje shared a bemused look.

"Anyhow," Eohne forged onward, speeding up. "I used these messenger bugs to help Jordan send a message to her father, Allan. Jordan was concerned because her mother went missing years ago and her poor dad would be sick with worry, because Jordan accidentally fell through a portal right after she and her father had a fight, and she hadn't been able to contact him to let him know that she's okay." Eohne took a breath and snatched a glance at Toth after this rapid delivery.

Toth took a swig of water from his waterskin. "I'm with you," he said, fixing the bag to his hip again. "Still not sure what it's got to do with me."

"Only half of my messenger bugs came home, at first I didn't know why." She faced him. "A little while later, the rest of them came home and I was able to extract data from the juice inside their bodies."

"Data?"

"Yes. The magic isn't important, what's important is that I was able to tell from the data that Allan followed the bugs through a portal."

Toth's face became drawn. "Jordan's father is here?"

"Yes."

"Does Jordan know that?"

"No."

"Where is he?"

"I believe he passed through into the desert."

"Which one?" Toth was growing more alarmed. It was clear he cared for Jordan, whether he admitted it or not.

"Saour Desert, south of Skillen."

Toth passed a hand over his face in aggravation. "That place is full of Willens and Gypsies. Bloodsucking little degenerates."

"Yes. And that's exactly whose hands he fell into," Eohne confirmed. "I believe they'll take him to Vischer. Probably to sell him, or turn him in for money."

Caje and Toth looked at each other. Caje crossed his meaty arms. "If they don't eat him."

"They might," granted Eohne. "But I refuse to accept that without trying to help him." Her chin jutted out stubbornly.

"There's only one place you're headed if you end up in Vischer," Caje ventured.

Toth nodded. "Trevilsom."

Eohne breathed out a sigh, relieved that the Nychts understood the danger Allan was in—more than that, they seemed to care.

"What's your plan?" Toth asked Eohne.

"Well, I came for your help. Obviously, my plan will change if you refuse to do so."

Caje's brow furrowed. "You know that we are under permanent contract with the people of The Conca? That we have commitments?"

"Yes, I know, but I thought…" She gestured toward Toth. "Under the circumstances—"

"He doesn't know Allan," said Caje. "And he only helped Jordan because she was wearing the indigo; she's not even a citizen of The Conca."

"I know that, too, but—"

"What kind of Strix is she?" Caje demanded, crossing his arms and raising his chin.

Toth had been meditating during this exchange but at this question, he interjected.

"It doesn't matter what kind of Strix she is," Toth said to his brother. He turned to Eohne. "Can you give us a minute, please?"

"Of course." Eohne went out through the fissure where they'd come in.

Caje and Toth looked at one another.

" 'It *doesn't matter* what kind of Strix she is'?" Caje echoed incredulously. "Since when doesn't it matter?"

"She's not from Rodania," Toth replied. "She isn't like them. She wasn't raised by them, brought up with their ideals, their prejudices."

"So you're saying she's probably Arpak."

"I have no idea. I'm just saying that if she is, I don't care."

Caje let a long breath out from his nose and watched as his brother turned the problem over in his mind. When Toth had returned from the job that had taken him outside of The Conca and to Charra-Rae, he'd done nothing but brood for days. When Caje had finally asked him what was on his mind, Toth had reluctantly told the story of rescuing two travellers from a harpy—in fact, the terrifying, overgrown matriarch who'd been killing horses south of Usenno. Caje had been overjoyed to hear that that particular harpy was dead, but Toth hadn't been in a celebrating mood.

Though Toth didn't admit it, Caje could tell that he'd come to care for the girl he'd rescued. In what capacity, Caje didn't know. Maybe he'd fallen in love with her. Maybe she reminded Toth of the sister they had lost all those years ago. It didn't matter. What mattered was that Toth cared for her, and whomever Toth cared about, Caje cared about, too. As he watched his brother brood, Caje knew what was holding Toth back.

"We'll cover your watch," said Caje. "Chayla and I. Go. We'll be fine."

Toth swung a grateful look his brother's way. "Normally, I'd protest that—"

"Normally, you wouldn't leave treaty territory. But you did. And whatever the reason, I trust it was worth it."

Toth nodded to his brother in silent thanks, Caje nodded back. It was decided.

The two Nycht brothers passed through the fissure, where they found Eohne fiddling with one of her blades and watching the skies as clouds rolled over the gorge. When she saw them coming, she sheathed her blade in one smooth motion without taking her eyes from Toth.

"You've had a lot longer to think this through than I have," said Toth to the Elf, as he separated from his brother. "Got any ideas?"

Eohne nodded. The two bent their heads together and squatted in the dirt and began to talk through a plan.

CHAPTER 14

Jordan bolted from the shop, the locket clutched in her hand. Belshar's shop was across the gap and, rather than taking the walkway and risking bowling someone over, Jordan hopped into the air. Her wings snapped out and she flew across the great divide between the streets, aiming for Belshar's towering, crooked offices.

"Sol!" Jordan yelled as she saw him exit the office tower. Her toes didn't quite find purchase on the edge of the sidewalk, and her wings flapped to catch her balance and right her.

Sol burst out laughing as Jordan's arms windmilled and her wings fluttered. Jordan joined in, although mostly because she was so excited; she didn't need any other reason to laugh. Sol reached out and grasped Jordan's hand, pulling her onto the walkway. Jordan fell forward into Sol's chest, he wrapped his arms around her to steady her. He looked around for the little blue dragon.

"Where's Blue?" Sol asked.

"Oh!" Jordan stopped laughing. "Blue! I forgot him in my hurry to come find you."

Jordan looked up into Sol's ice blue eyes and became

painfully aware of how close his face was to hers, how his arms were around her, his fingers brushing the feathers of her wings...

Sol let her go and stepped back, his tanned cheeks flushed with pink. "You forgot him?"

"Yes, I—" Jordan turned to face the gap she'd just flown across. "Ooooof!"

A flapping, squawking Blue barrelled into Jordan's stomach. She wrapped her arms reflexively around him and staggered backward into Sol.

Sol staggered back too, his arms wrapping around Jordan from behind. Jordan's yellow feathers blinded him and poked up his nose as Sol's right hand clamped down on something full and soft and warm. There was no mistaking the heavy softness of her breast, and heat rushed to Sol's face. His left hand accidentally wrapped around Blue's hind leg, and the dragon gave a whistle and nipped Sol's thumb. The staggering threesome collapsed in a jumble of limbs, feathers, and flapping leathery wings. Blue made an angry chittering sound as he hopped off Jordan's stomach and sat on his hindquarters in the dirt facing them. He might have been waving a ruler, for the way he looked like a teacher admonishing his pupils.

"I think he's telling me off," interpreted Jordan. "Oh, sorry!" she exclaimed as her elbow mashed Sol's hand into the stones.

Sol spat a feather out and pulled his booted foot from between Jordan's back and right wing. "It's okay. Not hurt."

More than a few Strix citizens and visitors chuckled at the clumsy tangle taking up half the walkway.

"Just a little embarrassed," Sol murmured, getting to his feet and holding out a hand to help Jordan up.

Jordan took great care in dusting herself off. Her face had a rosy tinge, and she found it difficult to meet Sol's eye. She cleared her throat. "The old artist was right."

"Who?"

"The artist I was just talking to. He said that Blue would always find me. I guess he was right."

"He knew about dragons, did he?" Sol straightened his satchels, which had become twisted around his torso.

"I guess." Jordan tucked stray hairs behind her ears. "Did you get to the bottom of the lapita problem?"

"Only a start," replied Sol. "Seems the new trade-master at Maticaw, some fellow by the name of Jack, is putting up roadblocks."

"Roadblocks *you* have to deal with?"

"Not me, thankfully. I told Belshar to go there in person."

"Oh, good. Hopefully he can get it sorted quickly." She brightened. "But, I have to tell you something amazing."

"Great. Not to rush you, but will it take long? My ring is heating up," Sol said, lifting a fist and showing Jordan his gold signet.

She peered at the ring. "I didn't know you had a ring. I never noticed it before." She found herself noting which hand and finger he was wearing it on, and was surprised by the relief she felt that it wasn't on the fourth finger of his *left* hand.

That's silly, she told herself. *They might not even have the same marriage rituals as we do on Earth.*

"Why is it heating up?" she asked.

"It's a signal from the palace that someone needs a courier. All couriers have a signet. When a message needs to be sent, the request is magically telegraphed to the rings. Until a courier shows up to take the commission, the rings get hotter and hotter."

"How hot do they get?" Jordan put a finger out and touched the gold. It was warmer than her skin.

"Hot enough to burn. We can take them off as long as we keep them somewhere we can feel them. Is it something you can tell me on the way back up to Upper Rodania?"

"I'll tell you right now," Jordan said quickly. "My mother is most likely in Maticaw." She didn't wait for this message to sink in. "I need to go back. Will you come with me?"

Sol's mouth opened. "Your mother...?" he gaped. "How do you know that? We haven't even gone to the census office yet."

"The locket. It's a compass," Jordan explained. She put her arms out for Blue, but he looked the other way. Jordan frowned at the reptile. "It drifted up from my neck when we were in Maticaw, and—"

"It did? You never said!"

"I didn't think it meant anything, and I was distracted by the gypsy lady, but—"

Sol put up a hand. "Come with me to Upper Rodania, tell me all about it and we can make a plan. I have to check in before my finger gets burned off."

"Alright," Jordan agreed. "Come on, Blue. You can be mad at me and still fly. Let's go, boy."

The dragon gave a growling yawn and flapped his wings, letting them know he was ready to go, albeit still annoyed.

The two Arpaks and the dragon took to the sky and began to climb.

* * *

THEY ARRIVED at the palace and landed on the same platform where Blue had last eaten.

"I won't be long," said Sol. "You must be getting hungry for lunch."

"No," protested Jordan, but at the thought of food, her tummy rumbled like a tractor. It was almost as though she'd had no breakfast.

Sol smiled. "You are. I am, too. And he definitely is." He pointed to where Blue had waddled underneath a chair and curled up again. "Let me see about this commission, and then we'll talk."

"Okay," Jordan sank into a chair and propped her elbows on the table.

She watched Sol disappear between the columns. Time to think always led to her parents. She wanted to locate her mother as quickly as possible, then go back home to Virginia and talk to her dad. She hadn't thought of what she was going to say, how she was going to break the news or even what her father might already know. After their argument, they never had the opportunity to have the talk—the one where he told her everything.

Is it possible he knows about Oriceran? Jordan's head shook at the idea. Surely her father would have told her *something*. He also had never seen the portrait inside the locket. *And what about in the longer term?* Passing through portals was supposedly dangerous and illegal—she shouldn't be making a habit of it. *But I'm an Arpak now; I've always been one. My home is really Oriceran. On Earth, I won't have wings.*

She fluttered her yellow feathers as though to remind herself they were still there. The weight of them was now a comfort on her shoulders, she couldn't imagine an earthbound life anymore. She frowned at the thought of living in a different universe from Allan. He was alone; it would kill him to lose her. It might kill her to lose him, too. *Would he consider living on Oriceran? Rodania is beautiful. But what would it be like for a human? Is my father too set in his ways to make such a huge move?*

Her mind wandered back to what Sohne had asked for—that the next time Jordan needed wings, she would seek Sohne out rather than some other source. Jordan wondered why, but it was just one of a thousand other questions jostling in her brain. All this thinking was exhausting.

Her eyelids had grown heavy by the time Sol emerged from between the marble columns. All the events of the past several days were taking a toll on her.

"What's the news?" Jordan asked, sitting up straight. "Did someone else get the commission before you?" She hoped so; she didn't want any delay in going back to Maticaw, and it would just be easier if Sol were with her. She was still so new to the ways of Oriceran and its many oddities and dangers.

"No, the commission is mine." Sol didn't look overly happy about it. "I'll have to leave first thing tomorrow. I have to pick up a letter from Prince Diruk and take it to Operyn."

"How far away is that?"

"Further than Maticaw. It'll take me about three days, if the winds are with me."

"Three days!" Jordan frowned. *Looks like I'll be going to Maticaw without Sol, after all. I can't wait three more days to find my mother.* "It's funny that you don't have some magical way of delivering mail instantly instead of ferrying it by hand. That's so much slower."

"There are ways, but the Elves have that magic, and it doesn't come cheap. King Konig and the Council members will sometimes pay for it if the message is really urgent. But it's not foolproof. They've had messages arrive jumbled, and misunderstandings can be embarrassing and expensive. They trust Arpak couriers—good thing, or I'd be out of a job."

Jordan nodded and rubbed her eyes with her fists. "Right."

"Come on," said Sol. "Lets go home and grab some food. I'm starved."

CHAPTER 15

It wasn't until their plates were clean and their glasses empty that Jordan said, "I've never been so hungry in all my life."

Sol smiled. "Better get used to that. Strix need a lot more calories than humans do." He took a breath before shifting topics. "So, I'll be back from Operyn in three days, then we can go to Maticaw together. If you like, I can give you directions to some of the sights of Rodania, so you and Blue can familiarize yourself with the city while I'm gone."

Jordan shook her head. "That's kind of you, but I can't wait three days to go back to Maticaw. I'll leave tomorrow morning; whenever you leave, that's when I'll leave. I'll meet you back here in three days, if that works for you." She brightened. "Maybe I'll have my mother in tow by then, you can meet her."

Sol's jaw went slack, and his ruddy cheeks paled. "Jordan, you can't go to Maticaw on your own. It's too dangerous. Even Arpaks who have been born and raised here don't make that flight by themselves."

"But," Jordan frowned. "My mother."

"She's been here for years, right?" Sol coaxed, moving forward in earnest. "What's a few more days? Besides, you don't know where to look."

"The locket will tell me."

"Yeah, but you have no idea where it'll lead you. What if it takes you out of Maticaw and into the wilderness somewhere?" Sol's tone was growing urgent. "Or into some nasty area of the city? I won't sleep for worry, Jordan!"

This last admission gave Jordan pause. She did what her father had told her to do during a conflict: put herself in Sol's position. If their roles were reversed, she'd worry about him—and he was much more capable than she was. The image of his frame crouched and waiting for the harpy attack in the dusty road of The Conca blossomed in her memory. He knew how to handle himself and he still hadn't won against the harpy; they'd had to be rescued. She might think she could take care of herself, but really? Against a harpy? She swallowed as she and Sol stared at one another. She could empathize with his feelings, but it didn't change the fact that she couldn't wait—she'd already waited too long. And a part of her resented the fact that she needed him.

"And what happens if you get back, and right away you have another commission?" she asked quietly.

Sol's lips parted, but he had no answer for that possibility. He closed his mouth and stared at Jordan, her blonde hair drifting around her face in the evening breeze.

His heart gave an unexpected ache.

"Please," he begged softly. "Please wait for me to return. I want to come with you." *It isn't just to keep her safe,* he realized. *She's about to find a mother she's never known and, no matter how romantic the notion is of reuniting with a long-lost family member, the whole situation doesn't seem right.*

Sol had no idea why Jaclyn would leave her baby girl on Earth and abandon Jordan's father, but it was the choice she had made. Unless there was some extreme circumstance that could justify the decision, it didn't make Jaclyn look good and Sol was worried about what Jordan might discover when she came face to face with her mother. *I want to be there for her.* He sat back in his chair as the final thought hit him like a punch in the heart.

"I'll have Blue," Jordan reminded him, breaking up Sol's thoughts like a ship cutting through ice.

Sol gave a disbelieving laugh. "He's a lizard! He'll be no protection for you."

An angry squawk came from the other room, and both of them jumped. They stared at one another with realization

"He understands us!" said Jordan. It seemed Blue had far better comprehension than any other animal Jordan had befriended, and she'd had a pony that put some of her human friends to shame.

"Apparently." Sol raised his voice and called out, "What are you going to do if a harpy attacks her, Blue?"

There was a whistle in answer and the scrabbling of claws on the wooden floor. Blue appeared from the bedroom door and stalked toward the terrace.

"Well?" Sol crossed his arms, waiting.

Blue drew his face back and gave a sort of hiccupping cough, followed by a snort.

"Yeah, that'll stop a harpy right in its—"

A jet of hot flame burst from the dragon's mouth. Sol and Jordan leapt up from the table on the terrace, as the blast of fire reached the wooden furniture and sent it up in a ball of flame.

"Blue!" Jordan cried, tripping over the chair in her effort to get away from the bonfire.

"Stop!" Sol yelled, his hands on top of his head in a comical display of shock.

Blue snapped his mouth shut and the flame died instantly. Smoke curled up from his nostrils and the corners of his mouth. The table was on fire and crackling merrily, sending smoke billowing up into the night sky.

Sol dashed into the kitchen and cranked open his water faucet to full blast. He grabbed a bucket from a closet and jammed it under the tap. "He's a fire breather?!" Sol almost danced in place as the bucket filled far too slowly.

Blue looked over his shoulder at Sol and Jordan thought that if a dragon could grin, that was what Blue was doing. Sharp white teeth glinted in the evening light as the dragon's lips pulled back from his teeth in a terrifying display.

"It's a good thing you're small," Jordan said to the reptile. "You're frightening."

Sol carried the full bucket to the terrace and threw it over the fire, dousing the flames with a loud hiss. He put the bucket down and stared at Blue.

"Sorry," Jordan said sheepishly, feeling responsible for her companion's behavior.

"I never liked that table anyway," Sol lied. He looked at Blue. "But can you not breathe fire in my apartment ever again, please?"

Blue yawned as if to say, *I make no promises*. He made his way back to the bedroom, where the dark underside of the bed awaited.

Sol narrowed his eyes at the dragon's back. "Does he look bigger to you?"

Jordan crossed her arms. "All the better to help protect me."

Sol raked a hand through his hair and looked at the smouldering pile of rubble on his terrace. "So he can breathe fire," he shrugged. "He's still no match for a harpy."

"Did you see the length of that flame? He could toast one alive from twenty feet!" Jordan claimed with no small amount of pride.

Sol groaned. "I'm too tired to debate with you any more about this. Will you at least sleep on it?" Sol was certain Jordan would see reason after a good night's sleep.

Jordan chewed her lip and considered this. "Alright." Truth be told she could use a bit more rest. "Unless you need it, I'm going to take over the bathroom. I smell like smoke."

Sol breathed a sigh of relief. "Take all the time you want."

* * *

JORDAN ROLLED OVER, a beam of morning light falling across her eyes and rousing her. She opened her eyes and smiled. *Today could be the day that I find my mother.* Jordan sat up and stretched. The answer was already in her mind. *I have to leave today, with or without Sol. There is no waiting.* She bounced out of bed and dressed. The sounds and smells of a meal being made were already emanating from the kitchen.

Blue appeared from underneath the bed and bumped his forehead against Jordan's calf with a whistle.

"Morning, Blue." Jordan crouched and took the dragon's blue face in her hands. She looked into his intelligent black eyes. "What do you think? Can we handle ourselves on a journey back to Maticaw?"

Blue's tongue snaked out and slapped Jordan across the chin in a reptilian kiss.

"I'll take that as a 'yes,'" Jordan decided, wiping her chin. She kissed the dragon on the nose and finished doing up her leather vest as she wandered from the bedroom into the kitchen.

"Smells good," she said, brushing her hair back and up, away from her face. She'd gone to bed with damp hair, and now had a crazy bouffant of curls. She raked up the mess and put it into a ponytail. "Morning. What can I do?"

"Morning. Want to make coffee?" Sol gestured to the stovetop espresso maker, which was more squat and fat than the Italian kind Jordan was used to. Sol shook the pan on the stovetop to toss the sizzling purple home fries. "Grounds are in the jar in the corner there."

"I'm so glad you have coffee here." Jordan filled the

coffeemaker with water. "Otherwise I'd go back to Earth, never to return."

Sol laughed but his chuckle had an edge. He watched Jordan out of the corner of his eye, still unsure of the outcome of their conversation the day before.

Jordan sniffed the coffee grounds and gave a sigh of pleasure. She filled the reservoir, twisted the coffeemaker closed, and set it over the spiral of small flaming jets—engineering that never would have passed safety tests back home.

Sol bent to check the frittata he had cooking in the belly of the stove. A delicious smell of eggs and vegetables blew into the room.

"Where's Blue?"

Jordan looked around and frowned. "He was just here." She shrugged and looked up at Sol with a guess on her face. "Hunting?"

Sol nodded and pulled the frittata out of the stove. He pulled two plates down and started toward the terrace. He stopped when he saw the blackened remainder of his patio table. He turned back toward the kitchen and set the plates and food on the countertop. "Guess we'll eat here."

Jordan poured the coffee then joined Sol in retrieving a couple of chairs, and they sat down to breakfast side-by-side. They picked up their forks.

"So." Sol cleared his throat. "About your trip to Maticaw…"

Jordan's eyes met his. "I have to go today. Please don't ask me to wait. I just can't."

Sol closed his eyes against her decision and let out a breath. "Jordan—"

"Of course I would rather you come with me, but…"

Sol looked at her. Jordan hated the sadness she saw there, the worry. "I won't stop you," Sol finally relented. He put his fork down.

"What about an escort?" Jordan offered. "In The Conca, Toth escorted us—"

"We're not in The Conca. Things don't work like that on Rodania. Toth is a rebel, a mercenary for hire. He has an agreement with the people living there." Sol put his elbows on the table and tented his fingers, thinking. "If you would agree to wait, I could probably arrange something with a Nycht from the palace guard who is off-duty, but—"

"I have to go this morning. As soon as we're done with breakfast, and Blue is back."

Sol's mouth was a grim line. "You do know that you're taking your life into your hands, right? There is a stretch of unprotected coastline you have to pass over between Rodania and Maticaw. By air, there are harpies; by land, there are any number of gypsies and bandits who think they own the forests. We didn't have any trouble on the way here because there were two of us flying together, but you'll be a solo female Arpak—"

"I remember the coastline," Jordan promised. "We'll fly fast."

"Blue isn't as fast as you are," Sol warned. "He could be a liability, even with his fire." Sol got up from the kitchen island and went to a tall wardrobe in the corner. He opened it and rustled around in the contents, pulling free a holster that held two foot-long, straight blades. "Take these. I regret that I haven't had any time to show you how to use them, but," he handed the holster to her. "Pointy side out, right?" He gave her a bleak smile.

Jordan got up from her chair and threw her arms around him. Not for the knives, but for the way he was not fighting her wishes anymore. Sol blinked with surprise before closing his arms around her, hugging her back, the holster dangling from a finger.

Jordan pulled back. "We'll be alright, you'll see." She dropped her eyes to the weapons. "Thank you." She took the gear and strapped it around her hips. "Don't suppose you have a gun instead?"

"I wish. We don't have tech like that on Rodania." Sol itched to put his hand against Jordan's cheek. The idea of something happening to her filled his belly with acid, but forcing her to stay was not in his nature. Being caged, physically or emotionally, was anathema to an Arpak—to any living organism, really.

"I'll fly with you until I have to turn north, and you have to turn south," he decided. "At least I can go with you that far."

Jordan nodded. "Okay."

A high-pitched whistle from the terrace drew the two Arpaks outside. Blue was perched on the railing, sniffing their breakfast out of the air. His belly was round with whatever he'd hunted down.

"Looks like you've eaten," Sol said to the dragon. "Hopefully not from the palace aviary, or there'll be hell to pay."

Blue squawked and hopped to the floor, the source of his breakfast a securely kept secret.

Sol put a hand on Jordan's back. "Let's finish breakfast. Then I'll show you a map, just to refresh your memory. I've got a compass you can take, too."

CHAPTER 16

The way the morning sunlight reflected on the ocean—waves capped with white and, beyond them, smooth blue—took Jordan's breath away. Jordan and Blue had spent the first half of the trip with Sol, stretching their wings, catching the ocean air currents, and enjoying the journey. Sol had been quiet, worried, not enjoying the journey as much as Jordan.

A line of dark in the distance became visible: the shore. This is where she needed to turn south and Sol needed to go north.

"Please be careful," he pleaded before they'd said goodbye. "Stay sharp. Don't daydream."

"I won't." She kissed Sol's cheek and hugged him as best she could while they hovered. "We'll be alright. You'll see." She put her hands on the hilts of the knives he'd given her. "I've got these, and Blue."

"See you in three days," Sol said, his mouth a grim line.

Once they'd parted, Jordan took the opportunity to try a few aerial tricks, dropping into a dive and tucking her wings back. She plummeted to the waves, the wind tugging at her hair and her stomach climbing into her throat. Trusting her wings, she skimmed across the tops of the waves, reaching out her hands to feel the spray before arching upward again to where Blue was peering down at her, watching her experiment.

Freedom. That's what this is. It's pure freedom.

I can't wait to fly with my mother like this. How surprised will Jaclyn be to see me? Does my mother still look the same as in those photographs on the mantel back home? Jordan let her mind wander as the miles of sea passed away below them.

She and Blue made a long curve to meet the cliffs and rocky beach, and followed it, keeping it on their right-hand side. Blue flapped steadily and silently along beside her.

The coastline was marked by a thin ribbon of pale sand that wound around the edges of endless rocky outcroppings; beyond that, as far as the eye could see, was wilderness. Patches of forest took turns with tundra, dotted by shallow water reflecting the sun. Bare rock jutted up in places, looking fuzzy with moss. The cliffs to the right dropped away from a sickening height to a harsh and inhospitable shore. Waves crested, rolled and smashed onto the rocks.

Jordan caught the smell of rotten meat just momentarily on the wind and wrinkled her nose, her heart galloping and her eyes darting around for signs of movement. But the scent passed, and their serenity remained. Their wings pumped, carrying them further south, and closer to Maticaw by the moment.

Jordan began to form part of a plan. First, find her mother. If Jaclyn was being detained somehow, or was in some terrible circumstance, as Jordan had imagined she was (*what else would keep Jaclyn away?*) then she'd need to be freed. Once her mother was rescued, they'd be free to pass back to Earth, back to Allan. They could all be reunited and, from there, they could make a plan together. Jaclyn and Jordan were Arpaks, native citizens of Oriceran. *Surely Allan will wish nothing other than to join us here and make a new life?* Jordan felt hope that her father could do something that he really loved here. *Maybe he can finally escape from politics.*

ASCENDANT

A piercing shriek blasted Jordan's eardrums, she gasped and cried out, her hands clamping over her ears. She looked at Blue, who was responsible for the cry. The dragon had his teeth bared and snapped them at the air, letting out another ear-splitting scream, which morphed into a roar.

With her hands still clamped over her ears, Jordan followed the dragon's gaze. Her heart hammered against her ribcage, rattling like it was desperate to get out.

A huge black shadow raced silently along the waves behind them.

Jordan's skin crawled with terror. *How did we not notice the harpy sooner? The beast fooled even Blue for how long?*

"Fly," Jordan exhaled to her companion. Both of them bolted forward, tripling their speed. Jordan began to curse herself silently, Sol's many warnings ringing in her ears. *Stupid girl,* she seethed. *What good will you do your mother if you're dead?* She grit her teeth and felt anger bubbling hot and hard in her chest. *No. I am so close to what I have wanted for so long. This overgrown vulture is not going to stop us.*

Tucking her chin into her chest and looking back between her feet was the best way to keep an eye on the monster. From this vantage point, the harpy was a sharp extended beak, two red eyes, long blunt horns pressed back against its neck, with a wingspan that made Jordan feel ill. Those wings pumped and the crimson eyes became clearer; the rough wattle hanging down from the throat swayed with the harpy's effort.

Jordan's hands flew to the handles of the blades Sol had given her. Her eyes darted to the cliffs whizzing by in a blur, looking for anything that could be used to help her and Blue escape.

Jordan's wings began to ache. She glanced at Blue, who was also laboring, yet she did not recognize any fear in the dragon's eyes. He had, however, begun to make a strange repeated sucking sound. His lips would curl back, revealing his razor-sharp teeth as he inhaled, then would close over them as he breathed out.

"Blue," Jordan gasped, but she had to save her breath; this was no time for talk. She glanced back again and her fear was made real before her eyes. The harpy was gaining. It was too strong of a flyer for Jordan and Blue to evade by simply running. Jordan's mind raced for an idea, a plan.

The cliffs blazed by, cracked in some places and sleek in others, sometimes reflecting the sunlight in blinding flashes.

The flyers zoomed by the openings of caves and dark fissures, but Jordan focused ahead rather than on the creepy vibe that poured out of the openings in the rock.

A gust of wind propelled them forward, and the stench of rotting meat burned her nose. She gagged and dipped lower, her wings faltering and then recovering. Nausea clenched at her stomach.

A shrill cry rose on the air behind them; the first cry the harpy had made. Jordan's insides iced up. It was a cry of triumph. Jordan wrenched the blades from their holsters, turning in the air to face the predator. She meant to scream out her own terrifying battlecry, but the sound quickly transformed into a wail of fear. There were two harpies. *Where did the other one come from?* The harpies snapped at one another, the recent joiner smaller and hornless. Jordan couldn't tell if they were arguing over who should make this kill, or if they were happy to see one another.

The answer became clear as the smaller harpy flew off to the left, away from the cliffs, and began to close in on Jordan and Blue from the side. Blue went on making that strange huffing sound, sucking in air, and his exhales were now accompanied with a groan.

Oh, Blue, Jordan's heart bled for her little reptile. *I was so foolish; I should have listened to Sol and waited. It is not worth dying for. I'm such a fool. I'm so sorry.*

Blue and Jordan banked away from the harpy on the left, toward the cliffs, until Jordan realized that they were being herded. *Of course,* she had a cold and miserable realization.

Harpies kill then let the meat rot for a few days before coming back to eat. How can a harpy eat her kill if the prey sinks below the waves and becomes fishfood?

"Stay over the water, Blue," Jordan panted. "Don't let them push us over land." The words came in gasps and Jordan wondered how long they could keep up this breakneck speed. Blue sounded like he was in increasing pain. *I have to do something.* She had at first been looking for some kind of shelter on the shoreline, but that was a mistake; the pair had to face these beasts over water, where they would hesitate to make a kill they would just lose. She gripped the hilts of the blades in her hands and prepared to turn and face her fate.

Then Blue let out a shrill shriek and banked toward the harpy on the left, sharp and sudden.

Jordan gasped, and even the harpy seemed to pull his head back with surprise at the dragon's sudden movement.

There was a loud snap, followed by a harsh blast of air, and the sky over the water seemed to explode with flames. The scent of charred, rotten meat replaced the usual harpy odor. There was a high-pitched wail of pain and the harpy on the left spiralled toward the waves like a plane shot out of the sky, trailing smoke. Flames billowed from his right wing and he hit the water at a high speed, skipping once over the waves. The fire was extinguished and the harpy looked like nothing more than a floating pile of kelp.

Blue flew back to Jordan's side and began to repeat the strange sucking sound. Jordan let out a relieved and shocked laugh *He was working up that blast of fire this whole time!*

But they were not in the clear yet. Furious at the loss of her companion—or so Jordan assumed—the remaining harpy gave a murderous roar. The sound of snapping jaws spurred Jordan and Blue forward.

"Think—" Jordan panted, "you can do that—" she sucked in another breath, "—again?"

Blue's response was another chugging heave of air as his lips pulled back from his teeth. He was going to try.

Jordan spied a strange dark blob on the coastline, an anomaly. She squinted at it but couldn't make out what it was. Jordan glanced back to see that it didn't matter what was ahead anymore; the harpy was upon them. Her beak was open and reaching for Blue. Jordan pulled up suddenly, wrenching her wings. She slashed at the face of the harpy. Its beak snapped closed and turned aside as her blade swiped harmlessly by. Jordan lost her momentum and dropped several meters. The harpy ignored her and drove for the dragon, her long sharp talons open and reaching.

"No!" Jordan screamed. Desperately, she threw one of her blades. It turned end over end, catching the sun once with a flash, and sailed by the harpy in an arch before plummeting toward the waves.

Blue made another snapping sound, but it wasn't nearly as loud as the first time. He turned to face the harpy, then let out a jet of fire into her face. The harpy barrel rolled to the side as the jet stream shot past. Jordan's heart turned to stone. The fire was less than half the strength of Blue's first blast, and the dragon's wings began to flag visibly. He began to lose height, and flapped erratically in an exhausted effort to stay aloft.

Jordan strained forward. She tossed the remaining blade from her left hand to her right and reached for Blue as he dropped. The harpy reached for him, too, her vicious talons opening.

"You can't have him!" screamed Jordan, infuriated by the satisfied look in the murderous demon's red eyes. Jordan slashed with the knife in her right hand and snatched at Blue with her left. The blade sliced across the hard, black, leathery skin just above the claw. The harpy snatched the claw back and turned to Jordan, her beak snapping fast and furious at Jordan's face.

Blue gave a sad whistle and fell away.

"You can die now, asshole!" Jordan screamed at the harpy,

baring her teeth and jerking her face back as its beak snapped in front of her nose. She jammed the blade up under the harpy's chin, where it got lodged in the thick wattle. With a powerful yank, Jordan pulled the blade out. The harpy gave a choked cry, and a stream of blood dribbled into the air.

She didn't know whether she'd made a killing blow or just given the harpy a minor flesh wound, but Jordan didn't care. She sheathed the bloody blade, tucked her wings in tight and dropped after Blue.

The dragon was fighting to stay above the water, his wings pumping weakly and out of sync. Jordan clenched her teeth and shot toward him, hoping she could reach him in time and bank away from the water—or they'd both end up in the waves. She reached out and grabbed Blue by the ribcage, shooting her wings out to catch the air. The weight of the dragon yanked on her arms, nearly pulling them both into the sea. She pulled with all her might as a shadow passed over them. Looking up, Jordan saw the harpy bleeding from her wattle while shaking her head. Then she looked down and spied them, her red eyes homing in on the pair now struggling just to stay aloft.

Oh no, Jordan thought helplessly. *She's going to pick us off like a couple of cherries.* She looked down at Blue. *Should I just drop him and hope he can swim?* It was the only thing she could think of, but no matter what her brain said, her hands would not let go of him; in fact, they pulled him tight against her chest. Blue let out an exhausted whistle and pushed the top of his head up under her chin as though to tell her it was okay, that they'd done their best.

The harpy dove.

Thunk!

A bolt streaked from nowhere, piercing through the ribcage of the beast. With a shrill scream, the massive harpy pinwheeled toward the sea. She passed by Jordan and Blue, her eyes now unseeing, and landed with a terrific splash in the waves. Salt spray hit Jordan in the face, and she heaved upward with Blue pressed to her chest. The base of her throat was burning from the screaming and the sucking back of air, but she grinned and screamed again, this time in relief and the triumph of the moment.

She glanced down at the dead beast, drifting and battered by waves, a single wing splayed out and blood pooling around her body.

"Take that," Jordan gritted out between locked teeth at the corpse.

Jordan's head was pounding with hot blood, and her eyes felt flinty with hatred. She squeezed Blue against her breast and closed her eyes, allowing herself a few breaths. Relief flooded her limbs and she suddenly felt weak and shaky. Looking around, she spied the same blob of gray on the shoreline that she had seen before, only now they were close enough to see that it was a tower. Whoever was manning that stronghold had just saved their lives. Jordan headed for the stone column with her dragon held tightly, safe in her arms.

CHAPTER 17

*A*s they neared, Jordan saw a Nycht get up on the stone ledge of the tower and straighten to his full height. He put his hand up in the air, his wings snapped open wide and then shut, opened wide and then shut again, signalling them. Behind him on the tower top was a huge crossbow, cocked upward.

Jordan released one arm from around Blue to wave back at him. A sparkling grin, visible even from a distance, broke out on the Nycht's tanned face. He put his hands on either side of his mouth and called something out in a foreign tongue. His voice was thick and smoky, with a rasp any blues singer would be proud of.

Jordan and Blue descended to the small tower platform to land beside the abnormally large crossbow. "Do you speak English?" She asked as her feet hit the stone. She bent and set Blue down at her feet. Blue immediately lay down, rested his chin on the stone, and curled his tail around his body.

" 'Course," the Nycht rasped, nodding.

"Thank you for saving our lives," Jordan said, folding her wings away and standing to hold out her hand. Her fingers trembled and her whole arm felt weak.

The Nycht grasped her hand firmly and shook it. "A handshake," he grinned. "Don't get to do that much. How quaint and human." He blew a breath out through pursed lips and shook his head. "That was the most spectacular display I have seen in all my time on the Towerhead. WUEEE!" The Nycht laughed and slapped his knee. "That just made all of the years here spent reading books and watching gulls shit in the ocean worthwhile. Name of Daws Urly. What name are you?"

"Jordan, and this is Blue," Jordan looked down at her exhausted dragon, whose shining black eyes were now barely open. "He's a hero," she said as the realization of what the small reptile had done for them flooded her with sudden emotion. She cleared her throat and got a hold of herself before she burst into tears and embarrassed herself. "You have a hell of a shot, soldier," she said, looking at the crossbow.

Daws put a hand on the metal side of the weapon and stroked it affectionately. "I can take the eye out of a breaching fish at a half-mile, and that's no lie."

Jordan spotted a familiar glyph, half-covered by Daws' finger. She took a closer look and a smile spread across her face. She shook her head in wonder.

"I met the person who made this," she explained.

The sight of the familiar stamp helped ground Jordan, and her heart seemed to settle back into something like its normal rhythm. Her knees still shook, though, so she leaned on the stone ledge behind her.

"Oh, yes?" Daws peered at the brand as though seeing it for the first time. "It was made in Skillen. I believe so, right."

"Maybe, but the engineer has a shop in Rodania."

Daws poked at the air and jerked his chin to the side for emphasis. "That would be the Lower or the Middle, most like."

"Yes, the Middle. She's a remarkable craftsman."

"Mhmm hmmm, to be sure," Daws agreed, but Jordan got the

feeling he was mostly being polite. He clearly didn't know Arth. "You know what else is remarkable, that there dragon of yours."

Jordan peered back at Blue, who was dozing with half his head tucked under one wing. A line of drool hung from the corner of his mouth and dribbled over the top of a claw. "Yes, he is."

"How much you want for him? Fellow like that would be a great addition to the Towerhead."

Blue cracked an eye open just a fraction, evidently still listening to their conversation.

"Oh," Jordan turned back to Daws. "He's not for sale. Blue has imprinted on me." *And I on him,* Jordan admitted silently. "We can't be separated. It would kill him." *Maybe it would kill me, too.*

Her new winged status had sealed her emigration to Oriceran, but even so, she still had the option to go home and resume her human life. Blue, however, couldn't go to Earth. Jordan realized right then that their fate was sealed. Oriceran was now her home for good.

"Kill him, huh?" Daws stroked his sandpapery chin. "Well, we can't have that, now can we?"

"No," Jordan agreed, looking back at Blue, who had shut his eye again. "So, you work for something called 'Towerhead'?"

Daws dipped his chin. "That's a yes. There's one hundred fifty-seven towers between here and the Skillen border. We guard the whole Maticaw shoreline." He swept an arm down the coast. "I'm the first tower on the north side, so you're lucky those hag-crows didn't sniff you out further up. There's nothing between here and Operyn. Nope."

"There's a sharpshooter at every tower?"

"Two, most times," Daws corrected her. "My partner went and got himself a case of the grippe." He chuckled. "Green as a troll's hair, he was."

"I'm sorry. That sounds awful."

Daws waved a hand. "He'll survive. Back tomorrow, more than like."

"He's a Nycht, too?"

" 'Course. We all are." He peered at her. "What did you say your name was?"

"Jordan. How did you get this job?"

"Well, my father was a Towerhead Nycht, and his father before, and so on. This job keeps you, not t'other way around."

"Did you ever want to do anything else?"

Daws looked struck by this question. "Why would I...?" he paused, his dark eyes blinking. He stroked his chin meditatively. "I guess if you're asking what I might do if I wasn't this," he opened his hands palms-up and shrugged his shoulders. "Why, maybe I'd help people some other way. Sewing up holes instead of making them, if you get what I mean."

"Like a doctor?"

Daws shrugged. "But what's the use? Things just are. And here I am," he slapped a hand on the crossbow.

Jordan spied a neat stack of books in the corner under an overhang. "You like to read when you're not watching the skies?"

"Oh, love it. Only when Howy is on watch, of course."

"May I?" Jordan gestured to the books, curious about what a Nycht of the Towerhead would read.

"Of course. I don't get many guests out here; you can set up a tent and stay for a year, if you want."

Jordan laughed. "Thanks for the offer." She picked up a few of the books and shuffled over the covers one at a time. "These are in four different languages?" She looked up at Daws, impressed. "You know four languages?"

"Seven," he replied matter-of-factly.

Her jaw went slack. "You speak *seven* languages?"

"Speak?" He knocked his head side-to-side, indicating *maybe, maybe not*. "Predoian is particularly difficult to speak. I can read it fine, but that gargling in the back of the throat..." He put his fingers to either side of his windpipe. "Tough to master."

"Still. Seven! Where did you learn seven languages?"

"Seven's not so many," Daws said, blushing and looking uncomfortable. "Howy speaks twelve."

"What?"

"We grow up speaking Rodanian and some kind of English; there's a few different dialects, so it depends what our parents learned." He began to count off on his fingers. "Howy taught me Baldanese, I learned Predoian from that book there. My mom taught me Lakterin, because that's where her parents were from, and I learned German and Italian from books." He held up his fingers. "Seven. But Howy also speaks—"

"Wait, wait, wait. You speak German and Italian? Those are Earth languages."

Daws nodded, his brows drawn as if he was waiting for her to make a point.

Jordan spluttered. "But where did the books come from? What good are those languages to you?"

"Earthlings immigrated here, didn't they, before the Great War. Earth languages aren't uncommon to this day on Oriceran. No harm in learning them, even if they've changed somewhat." Daws waved his hand in a way that was becoming familiar to Jordan. "Books are easy to come by. The books aren't illegal; just the passing back and forth of them are, and I've got nothing to do with that. German and Italian are both fun to speak, they keep my brain sharp."

"That's why you learned them?"

Daws shrugged. "More or less. But maybe there's a part of me that hopes to meet up with someone from Earth one day, and if that happens, I'd like to be able to talk to them. Not just a descendant of an Earthling but an actual current-day resident. You know?"

Jordan nodded as she gazed at the Nycht with something like wonderment. "You could be a translator."

Daws flashed that big, good-natured grin of his. "Not much use for translators on the Towerhead, Jordan. A sharp eye, good aim, and some aerobatic capability are what matter here." Daws' eyes dropped to Jordan's chest, and his grin slowly faded. He pointed to his own chest, "Something wants your attention."

Jordan looked down and saw that the locket was turning and flopping weakly against her breastbone. "Oh!" She gave a gasp. "It's working!" She handed Daws his books, her wings had begun to flutter impatiently. "It's nice to have met you, Daws," she said, shaking his hand again. "I have to go. But thank you again, so much, for," she gestured at the now peaceful sky, "you know."

"Anytime, Jordan. Anytime. You're dancing like you need to make water." He gestured into the trees behind the tower, "There's a privy in the bush over there."

"No, it's not that." *Though, come to think of it, I could actually make use of a bathroom after the fright we endured.* "I'm just looking for someone, and," she grasped the locket in her fist, "this is my signal that I'm close."

"Alright then," Daws smiled. "Come back and visit anytime. It gets mighty lonely up here on the Towerhead. Howy will sure be mad that he missed meeting you."

"Well, tell Howy I said hello, and that I've never met anyone who can speak twelve languages. That alone is worth coming back for."

Daws' grin widened, but Jordan didn't think he saw the whole poly-linguistic ability as being quite as impressive as she did.

"Oh," he said as she woke Blue up and set a foot up on the edge of the tower. "Try not to fly back to Rodania on your own. That's where you came from isn't it?"

"Yes."

"I know you have him," Daws nodded at Blue. "But these skies are dangerous right now, and they seem to be getting more dangerous by the day." His dark eyes became serious. "Have you got someone you can fly back with?"

"Maybe." Jordan was hoping that that 'someone' would be Jaclyn.

"If not, it might be worth paying for an escort if you can."

"I'll keep that in mind. Thanks, Daws." Jordan crouched beside Blue. "Have you got anything left, little buddy? We can't stay here for the night." Blue raised his head and blinked solemnly at her. He huffed a sigh and got to his feet, half-opening his wings. "Good dragon." Jordan put her hand on his back. "I promise we'll rest soon. We're close now."

Jordan stepped up on the tower edge and Blue crawled up beside her.

"Good travels, Jordan."

"Thanks, Daws. Good luck to you." Jordan gave their new friend one last smile.

Jordan and Blue lit into the air. She waved back at the lonely figure on the tower. His elbow was resting on top of the deadly crossbow as he watched them resume their journey south.

CHAPTER 18

By the time Blue and Jordan descended into the streets of Maticaw, the locket had taken on more life and was floating halfway between her chest and her chin. Without knowing where to start, Jordan headed for Cles's tower—the only familiar place to her in Maticaw. She and Blue landed in the busy market street not far from where they'd first met.

"Recognize the place, Blue?" Jordan asked her reptilian companion.

He bumped against her calf with his forehead and plopped down, exhausted.

Jordan spied a crumbling clock tower, from which she learned it was just after three in the afternoon. Her stomach rumbled, and she knew for certain Blue had to be hungry, too. They explored the market until a delicious smell drew them to a small kiosk where Jordan bought two enormous flatbreads wrapped around dripping cooked meat and vegetables. She and Blue wandered into a small park and sat down on the grass for their picnic.

If Blue had a preference for food he'd caught himself, he didn't show it. The dragon tore through his wrap, wolfing down the meat and the veggies, but only picking at the bread once he'd finished all the rest. He drank his fill from a small fishpond and came back to curl up at Jordan's side. Jordan finished every last morsel of her own meal and lay back on the grass for a rest. She watched her locket through half-closed eyes as it bobbed weakly at her neck. They dozed as the shadows grew longer and the air grew humid and cool.

Jordan finally roused Blue, who seemed much better after his meal and nap. They both rose and stretched. Jordan knew they'd both be sore the next day—probably for the next few days.

"So, where to?" Jordan murmured as she reached down to stroke Blue's head, gazing at the locket. It wasn't really offering a precise direction—more just floating there in the air. They left the small park as the clock tower chimed six, and began to walk.

The crowds had dwindled as the dinner hour drew close, but they still had to skirt Arpaks, Elves, and goodness knew what other species. From the corner of her eye, Jordan saw a short, fat man whose skin had the color and shine of mercury. She looked away even though she really wanted to stare.

The dust and noise of the busy marketplace swallowed them up. Jordan kept her eyes on the locket, watching to see if its behavior would change. When they passed an intersection in the street, the locket swayed left.

"This way, Blue." Excitement was building in her belly. She could hardly keep her hands from shaking and her eyes from misting up. Her mother was not far away; they could be upon her in a matter of minutes.

The locket led them downhill toward the harbor. Clouds were gathering on the horizon, muting the sun's rays as it swung lower and lower toward the water. Broad stone stairs led them past level after level of city streets. Looking left and right as they passed through intersections, Jordan spied all manner of blade signs for shops and services as well as what looked like gateways into private residential buildings, all hidden away behind walls smothered with vines and moss. The air grew increasingly cool and humid. They paused at a landing where a low brick wall cut off their progress. The locket, clearly unaware that there was no passage over the stone wall, kept tugging toward the water. The pull was stronger now, and the chain pressed into the skin on the back of Jordan's neck.

"Let's fly, Blue," suggested Jordan, propping a foot up on the short retaining wall. "It'll be faster than wandering the streets, and it seems like we need to go down to the harbor."

They took to the air and flew lazily over the city, toward the port. Multi-masted sailing vessels of all sizes, shapes, and colors drifted in and out. Tiny people ran to and fro on their decks and up and down the rigging as they either prepared to dock, or prepared to set sail. Less often, some strange-looking airship droned overhead to some unknown destination, or even hovered over the water, probably by magic. Still, the locket tugged Jordan toward the water.

Maticaw's port was a congested and active place. The stench of oil, the fug of smoke, and the heady fragrance of spices filled the air with a thick confusion of scents. Several parallel docks stretched out into the water and were crowded with vessels and people running about, carrying this and that, unloading and loading. Barrels were rolled; boxes and crates were pushed on carts, or magically winged through the air on platforms; smaller, more ornate trunks and cases were carried carefully by hand. Some of the humans and other species working in the port were dressed in elaborate clothing, but most were dressed in plain, homespun outfits. Almost everyone carried a weapon of some kind. Many of those at work were Arpaks and Nychts—some of them armed to the teeth and terrifying to behold. Jordan felt almost as though she'd fallen into the Caribbean, during the days of pirates and privateers.

She and Blue landed on a wooden boardwalk that followed the coast and linked the docks. Broad bays in between the docks were choked with vessels of all sizes, drifting, docked, or navigating the mess of traffic as best they could on their way in or out of port.

The locket continued to pull Jordan out to sea, tugging at her neck with more strength. There was nothing there except for ships. *Is my mother on one of the vessels in the harbor?* Jordan followed the locket's trajectory, which didn't seem to be pointing to any particular ship. "This makes no sense," murmured Jordan, scratching her head.

A burly fellow with a carpet balanced on his shoulder spied the confused Arpak woman. "Trouble, miss?" He was a barrel-chested man with a bald head and kind eyes.

"What's out there?" Jordan asked, pointing out at the horizon.

"You don't know?" the man's brow wrinkled. "Rodania. You're Arpak; it's your city, and you don't know where it is?"

She frowned. "No, I know where Rodania is, I just…" She blinked down at the locket and wrapped her hand around it. "Is there anything else?"

"Trevilsom prison is beyond Rodania, and after that, nothing but miles and miles of ocean until you reach Potakwa." He gave the kind of suspicious side-eye that Jordan was beginning to grow weary of. "Where are you from?"

She sighed. "Thanks for your help." She mustered a smile for the kind stranger. "I'm looking for someone, and this…" she held up the locket, "…tells me that she is out there." She pointed at the horizon. "But it's just pointing out to sea. The locket would only work if she were close by, so she can't be all the way across the ocean, and it's not pointing at any of the ships. Can you see my dilemma?"

"Maybe at the trade office?" the man offered with a doubtful look.

"Trade office?"

"Aye," he said. "It's a small island not far off the coast. The mist makes it hard to see sometimes. It's just there," he pointed a finger the size of an American hot dog.

Jordan peered out at the horizon. He was right; there was a small something swaddled in cloud that, if one didn't look closely enough, could easily be missed. Jordan's heart resumed its excited thrum as she let go of the locket. It drifted forward and strained at her neck in the direction of the shadowy blob nearly swallowed by fog.

"Thank you," Jordan shot a huge grin at the stranger. "I would have totally missed it."

"Welcome," he said, bobbing his head humbly. He shifted the carpet to get a better grip and said, "Luck to you," before lumbering away.

* * *

THE TRADE OFFICE might more aptly have been called 'Trade Rock'. A dark gray mess of rock slabs, piled high like a messy jumble of books, jutted up from the water. The slabs made a kind of layered tower on one side of the island. On the other side, clusters of modular buildings emanated light from small, round windows. In the center, a fortress had been carved out of what looked like a single large block of granite. A sturdy, handmade, wooden sign on posts with carved out letters had been driven into the black sand on the narrow beach. The sign was long and very tall, because it listed 'Maticaw Trade Office' in what must have been nearly twenty languages; there were too many to count at a glance.

Jordan and Blue landed on the small strip of beach, the black sand swallowing up the soles of Jordan's boots. The locket was now pulling hard enough to bite into Jordan's neck and make her wince. Jordan took it off and held the locket in her fist instead. It surged forward behind her fingers.

"We're close, Blue." She gazed up at the huge stone building.

"So close now." She walked up the beach. Blue gave a squawk and flapped his wings, making Jordan turn. He took to the air after some sea bird, and Jordan watched him fly up into the mist and disappear.

"When you gotta eat, you gotta eat," she murmured, feeling suddenly bereft. She trudged onward. The sand became slabs of off-kilter rocks, which became steps. She climbed them to the base of the fortress. It now took real effort to hold the locket, and she wrapped the chain over her hand to help her grip it. She took a deep breath through her nose. *My mother is in this building.*

The fortress loomed, and Jordan shivered at a cool gust of wind that cooled her neck and ruffled her hair and feathers. A huge wooden door, both tall and wide, sat askew, like a shutter on a haunted house. Not sure what the protocol was, Jordan knocked on the wood. The sound from her knuckles was dull and quiet and not likely to be heard by anyone not holding their ear on the other side.

Jordan grasped the large iron handle, the metal ice cold under her hand. She pulled, and the heavy door opened a crack and then banged shut again, pulling free of her hand. She yanked with more strength, and the door swung heavily and silently open. She stepped inside and propped the door open with her back, bracing her legs against the concrete floor. Her eyes worked to adjust to the gloom.

"Hello?"

The sound of her voice echoed into the empty blackness. Cool, stale air touched her skin, smelling of dust and moldy grain. She called out again, cocking her ear to listen. The place felt like a tomb. She stepped inside and took a few tentative steps forward. The door banged shut behind her and darkness swallowed her. She waited until her eyes adjusted and caught sight of a dim glow from cracks in a door far ahead of her. The door appeared to be hovering several feet off the floor.

Jordan called out for a third time; no response. She walked

forward and her eyes adjusted further. She could just make out a short set of steps leading up to the door.

"Ouch!" she banged her shin on something sharp and bent down to feel the corner of a cold metal shelf. The locket pressed against her fingers, directing her onward.

There came the scuttling sound of tiny, clawed feet, as some small animal panicked and scrabbled for cover. The shapes of crates and bags came into focus, stacked in haphazard piles and clusters on the floor. She reached the steps and ascended, turning sideways and ducking through the small passageway, which had clearly not been built to accommodate Strix. She reached out for a handle and found a jutting piece of metal. She followed it to the cold iron latch, which she lifted. The door swung easily and silently toward her. She took the final step up and passed into the light, letting the door close behind her.

Jordan found herself standing on the periphery of a fantastic hallway. An ornate red carpet threaded with gold ran the length and breadth of the hall. Glass sconces lit the way, and huge, elaborate paintings of landscapes far too large to appreciate properly in a hallway had been hung on the gray stone walls. Rustic wooden furniture—chairs and tables topped with vases stuffed with tall ornamental grass—warmed up the space.

The locket strained behind her fingers, begging Jordan to walk through the wall in front of her. Taking in the opulence of the broad corridor, Jordan shook her head. From the outside, the building looked like a drafty fortress; from the inside, it looked like a gallery.

A woman who would look completely at home in any corporate boardroom in America appeared from around the corner at the far end of the corridor carrying a stack of papers. She had dark-rimmed glasses perched on the end of her nose and red hair swept back into a tight professional-looking ponytail. She wore a pencil skirt, a button-up blouse and a matching vest with a small silk bow at the throat. She was reading one of the pages in her arms rather than watching where she was going, taking small steps in black pumps. Jordan was so surprised to see someone looking so like an Earthling that she just stared at the woman. The businesswoman blinked up at Jordan briefly as she passed by, gave a demure smile without really looking at her, then looked down at her paper and carried on.

Jordan watched the woman sway down the hall, completely bemused. She strode after her. At the end of the hall, the woman turned left, and the locket tugged Jordan right.

She turned and carried on.

The locket urged her to walk through the wall on her right. *There has to be a room on the other side of these walls.* The hallway was warm and Jordan's brow began to feel damp and sticky with moisture. The hall suddenly came to an end and a cavernous room opened before her. A small desk sat in front of a tall, narrow window, behind which another professional looking woman sat. She was scribbling furiously into a ledger with a pencil. She too was dressed in corporate clothing, but she was younger and plumper than the lady Jordan had passed in the hallway. Her fingernails were painted a pretty shade of pastel green and her eyeshadow matched. Her blonde hair was swept up in a tight bun and small diamond earrings sparkled from her earlobes.

The locket strained away from the girl and toward a set of enormous double doors opposite the desk. Upholstered chairs sat clustered together in front of a cold fireplace, unused and looking like the staged set of a talk show.

The young woman looked up at Jordan and greeted her in what the new Arpak was beginning to recognize as Rodanian.

"Pardon me, I speak English only," apologized Jordan.

The girl smiled a bright welcoming grin at her, as though meeting someone from her hometown far across the world. "And beautifully," she complimented. "You almost sound American."

Jordan bit off the 'I am' that surged to her lips, and instead said, "I'm looking for Jaclyn Kacy. Do you know her?"

The smile froze on the girl's face. It was as though she had turned into marble.

Through bared teeth, she replied, "Jaclyn?" in a very uneasy tone of voice. Her eyes darted to the doors behind Jordan and then back to Jordan's face. Her previously rosy cheeks lost their color.

"Is something wrong?" Jordan's palms felt clammy. The girl's reaction was not comforting.

"Um." The pencil in the girl's fingers dropped to the tabletop with a clatter, she snatched it up again and fiddled with it. "How do you know Jaclyn?"

She said 'Jaclyn' in a hard, sharp way, loading the name with meaning. Jordan swallowed with an audible click, her throat was dry.

"She's my mother."

The girl pursed her lips and tilted her chin down to peer at Jordan over the tops of her specs. The film of ice that had formed at these words was so palpable that Jordan gave a little shiver.

"Right," the girl replied. She laid the pencil carefully in the seam of the open ledger. "That's a new one." She pushed her chair back from the desk and stood, her movements stiff.

She lowered her voice a notch but still spoke with authority. "I'm afraid I'll have to ask you to leave. Quietly. I'm not sure who has put you up to this, or what they're paying you, but—believe me—it's not worth it. You need to go, before you get into a situation you can't reverse." The girl's green eyes darted again to the large doors behind them; the same doors the locket was straining toward.

Jordan was aghast at this. "Why would someone pay me to—?"

"There is no Jaclyn." The girl said this flatly, as though the phrase had been drilled into her head so many times, it had become meaningless. The girl placed her fingertips on the tabletop, making two little spiders with her fingers. She leaned forward. "For your own good, miss." Her eyes actually turned pleading, and her voice dropped to a whisper. "Go away, and don't come back." Her pupils darted to the door once again and then back to Jordan, wide and desperate. "Please," she hissed.

A confused fear struck at Jordan's heart, but she steeled herself. She lowered her voice in response to the girl having done so. "I have come a long way to find my mother." She showed the girl the locket, keeping a tight hold on it. She clicked the small latch with her thumb and it snapped open, revealing the portrait inside. "I *know* she's here. This locket led me to her. Against all odds, in the face of the years that have separated us..." Jordan's voice began to tremble. "If you don't let me through those doors, I will let myself through."

The girl's eyes widened to the size of teacups as she looked at the artwork in the locket. "Where did you get that?" she wheezed, a hand flying to her throat.

Jordan snapped the locket closed and clenched her fist tightly around it. "Doesn't matter. Are you going to let me in?"

"I can't!" The girl looked agonized and put a hand out toward Jordan. "You don't want to go in there."

"Oh, but I do." Jordan clenched her teeth and turned toward the door, striding across the carpet, her footsteps silent.

There was a scuffle behind her as the girl came around the desk and chased her across the room. A freezing cold hand wrapped around Jordan's bicep. The girl pulled Jordan to a stop.

"Don't," she whispered, and stepped in front of Jordan. She put her other hand on Jordan's shoulder and began to push Jordan back the way they'd come, angling her toward the hallway. "I can't explain it, but I'm doing you a favor right now. Besides, the door is locked; you can't go in unless you're invited. I have no key." She said the last word softly and conspiratorially, as though she was now on Jordan's side and Jordan should trust her.

"This is ridiculous." Jordan resisted the girl. "I'm going in there, one way or another. I have come too far to—"

There was a loud *click*, and one of the double doors swung open.

The secretary uttered the shocked squeak of someone who's been caught stealing. She snatched her hands away from Jordan, and whirled to face the open door. She plastered a stiff look of calm and serenity on her face; the result was a rictus of doll-like fear.

In the doorway, surprise passing over his face at finding a woman and an Arpak standing awkwardly close together, was a tall and golden Arpak man. The surprise faded as quickly as it had come, and a cool disinterest took its place. The Arpak's feathers looked as though they'd been dipped in gold. They glittered uniformly, with no distinct markings or pattern, and reflected the firelight from the sconces along the wall. His cool beauty made Jordan take an involuntary step back—which was good, because the girl also stepped back, the two of them moving in tandem. His skin was pale and freckled, his hair so blonde it was nearly white—the color of summer wheat. He was tall and lanky, with a long torso. A black velvet vest with gold piping wrapped itself snugly across his chest, belted at the waist with thick, black leather. A single dagger with an obsidian hilt glittered from his right hipbone, and black leather pants encased his long slender legs. He oozed wealth and superiority. His cool, dark blue eyes fell on the secretary, then on Jordan, and skipped over them the way a stone skips over water. He breezed by, leaving a pleasant, spicy aroma in his wake.

The heavy door began to swing shut; Jordan saw her opportunity. While the girl was still ogling the beautiful Arpak male, Jordan dashed around her and darted through the shrinking gap. Her feathers just slipped through behind her. The last thing she heard before the door slammed shut was a gasp from the secretary and the word "No!" expelled on a sigh of terror.

CHAPTER 19

As the door banged shut, Jordan halted just inside, her face a mask of shock. The locket pulled free from her fingers and flew across the room.

Jaclyn, who had been bent over a large wooden desk, looked up and gasped with surprise. A hand flashed out, as quickly as a striking cobra. The locket slapped against her palm, hard, and her fingers closed around it. An Arpak man who had been bent over the same desk straightened, his mouth agape, his eyes on Jaclyn's hand. One of his hands flew reflexively to the hilt of the blade at his hip.

Jordan forgot to breathe as she took in her mother's appearance. She just stood there, her back to the door, her heart hammering in her chest, and her vest feeling as restrictive as a straightjacket. Her torso felt hot and prickly, but her feet and hands felt cold as ice.

Jaclyn was even more beautiful than all the photographs in the Kacy parlor showed. Her hair was no longer long and curled, but bobbed and hooked back behind her ears. She was tall and willowy; her every line and curve screamed femininity. Her thick-lashed, chocolate-brown, doe eyes, now graced with fine-lines, were dressed in subtle makeup that made them look even larger. Her cheekbones were dusted with peach blush and small black pearls glittered from her ears. She wore a long-sleeved wine-colored shirt with quilted lines stitched into a diamond pattern and a snug pair of black leather pants. The foot that Jordan could see peeking out from behind the desk wore a tall, laced-up boot with a low heel and stitched flourishes across the toe. Jaclyn's olive skin was pale, as though she hadn't seen the sun in a long while. The overall impression Jaclyn gave was one of competent glamour—a high-achieving, high-society commander.

Jaclyn's fist remained frozen in the air, clenched around the locket. Her eyes tracked from the locket to the woman at the door. Her fist slowly lowered. Jaclyn's eyes narrowed. With a fast, bird-like movement, Jaclyn looked down at the locket in her hand. Her expression showcased that she'd seen it before, but maybe not in a very long time. She didn't open it, but looked back up at Jordan, her head tilting.

"Where did you get this?" Jaclyn's voice was soft in the way a wolf's pelt is soft—cloaking a dangerous, predatory imperative beneath it. She put a hand out toward her companion as though to say, *'relax'*.

Jordan's body remembered that it needed oxygen to live and she finally took a breath. Jaclyn's question had sailed by unheard, for Jordan was in shock about something else entirely. Words finally found their way out, bursting like they, too, needed air desperately.

"You're not Arpak!" The one thing Jordan had been expecting was conspicuously absent—wings. "Or did you just recently return from Earth?" Jordan thought that her own voice sounded small, wounded.

The change in Jaclyn's face was subtle, but belied a moment of monumental realization. Maybe it was Jordan's voice, or something in her face that reminded Jaclyn of Allan, maybe the way her mouth moved when she spoke. Jaclyn's generous lips parted with a soft intake of breath.

"Jordan," she breathed, recognition changing the landscape of her face and dropping her shoulders. Her eyes turned glassy as she stared at her daughter.

"Mom?" Jordan took a few tentative steps forward, but stopped when Jaclyn made no move to welcome her. Emotions pelted Jordan: confusion, happiness, excitement, unease, bewilderment, disbelief; she felt like a cocktail of substances that should never be mixed.

The Arpak man, whom Jordan had barely registered, covered his mouth with a hand and stared at Jordan. His eyes darted from one woman to the other and then settled back on the Arpak with the yellow wings standing in the middle of the room. He dropped his hand.

"How did you get in here?" he barked, his voice a low growl.

Jordan finally looked at him. "I walked in through the basement." She looked back to her mother. "I'm sorry, I didn't know how else to find you. I just followed the locket." As she spoke, she realized that the Arpak with her mother was young—maybe only early-twenties—but he was armed like Toth had been. The hilts of multiple weapons gleamed from their leather sheaths. He moved with a liquid grace as he stepped around the desk. He had soft, unlined skin and a rosy, youthful complexion, untouched by loss and years. He rested a palm on the hilt of a blade, his weight shifting forward onto the balls of his feet, as though preparing to come at her. He had light gray wings with soft orange primary feathers, and long, dirty blonde hair tied back. There was something familiar about his face. Jordan wondered if he was related to the other blonde man who had left the room only minutes before. His eyes were hard and glowered at her.

"Ashley," said Jaclyn, her tone sharp. The man looked at her. Jaclyn's look was withering and the Arpak bared his teeth in what seemed to Jordan the look of a cowed dog. The tension in the room was palpable.

Should I be afraid? Maybe the girl's warnings had been sincere, but Jordan hadn't come all this way to chicken out. Being afraid of her own mother seemed ridiculous, unthinkable. *My mother is sweet, nurturing, a soft-heart...isn't that what everyone has told me since I was little?*

Jordan took a step forward, her eyes on Jaclyn. "You left us. You left me without a mother. Why? What happened to you?"

"If you take another step—" the Arpak man hissed.

"Ashley," warned Jaclyn, putting a hand on his arm. Her knuckles were white. "She's not here to hurt me."

"She *knows* now," Ashley replied. "She's seen you."

"It's not yet clear what she knows," answered Jaclyn, her eyes locked on Jordan.

Confusion and despair snuck up behind Jordan and wrapped around her in a long, slow, creeping hug. *None of this is making sense;* not Jaclyn's reaction, not the exchanges between her mother and her mother's guard, not this strange and ornate office where she'd found her, not the fact that she was on an island off a port used solely for handling trading vessels as they passed in and out of Maticaw. It was bizarre. And to add to the confusion, it was pretty clear that Jaclyn was in charge here.

Jordan did take another step but Ashley stayed where he was, with Jaclyn's hand still on his arm.

"What are you *doing* here?" Jordan demanded, her voice rising a little. Anger began to burn in her gut as the shock began to pass and made way for her assumptions to spill forth. "I thought I'd find you in some dangerous circumstance, thought maybe you were being kept against your will. What else would keep you from your family? I thought you were Arpak!" Jordan cried this last one out, loud and forlorn. "Why else would you leave your baby? You never even left a note. Do you know what a mess you left behind you? Do you even care?" Jordan's heartbeat pounded strong and loud, like a warship's drum as its oars worked to carry it to ramming speed. She fought to steady herself and made fists to stop her fingers from trembling.

"Here you are," she went on. "Human, and—and what?" Jordan looked around at the room: tall ceilings, rich-looking upholstery and furniture, bookcases and shelves full of documents, scrolls, and ledgers. An elaborate chandelier hung down from the ceiling, illuminating the room. Three tall doors led off to goodness knew where and there were no windows in the room, not one. It was a beautifully furnished cell and clearly a place where business was done. "You're a CEO or something? On Oriceran? Is *this* what you abandoned your family for?"

Jaclyn crossed her arms over her chest. "You don't have a clue what you're talking about," she accused, her voice icy. "If I thought I could raise you and also do what I was meant to do, I would have. But it would have killed Allan for me to take you away. I was being kind."

" 'Kind'!" Jordan spluttered. "We're your *family*!" She was losing the fight with her emotions. Her nose tingled, the edges of her vision grew blurry and her sinuses felt like they were filling up with her brains. "We needed you. I needed you." Jordan's voice hardened. "What kind of a woman leaves her family—"

"Clearly you didn't need me," interrupted Jaclyn calmly. She gestured to Jordan's wings. "I see you've discovered your heritage." Her beautiful face softened as she gazed at her daughter. "Perhaps that is for the best. It will force you to take a side."

"Take a side?" Jordan echoed. The room went fuzzy. Jordan's hands went to the sides of her face and pressed there, as though to keep her skull from falling apart. She squeezed her eyes shut. *This is agony.* Jordan couldn't have felt more gutted, more disappointed, more shocked, than if the armed Arpak had run her through with one of his blades.

"It nearly killed Dad," she choked out through a tight jaw.

"What?"

Jordan opened her eyes and glared at Jaclyn. "You leaving. It nearly killed Dad. You have no idea what you put him through."

Jaclyn scoffed. "Allan most definitely never needed me."

"It broke him when you left! He loved you!" A tear slipped free. Jordan brushed it away angrily.

"Love?" Jaclyn looked surprised at the mention of such a thing in tandem with her husband. "A meaningless word representing an even more meaningless sentiment." She waved a hand dismissively.

Jordan didn't miss the hurt and surprised look that Ashley shot Jaclyn; it was there and gone, just a shadow passing over his face. *He might not just be her guard,* Jordan realized.

Horror crawled over her skin and raised gooseflesh in its tracks. *What was it Dad said to me the last time we fought? It was one of the last things he said before he left the house. I demanded he tell me everything about Jaclyn and the locket, everything and anything I didn't already know. What had been his response? 'Even if it makes you hate her?'*

"If you're not Arpak, how am I Arpak? Unless you are, and you just came back from Earth?" Sol had said that wings would grow back on their own, given enough time on Oriceran.

Sol. The thought of him made Jordan's heart ache. How she wished for his solid companionship now. *I've never felt this vulnerable.*

"This isn't good. I don't like this," Ashley muttered and shifted from one foot to the other, toying with the hilt of the blade at his hip. He was studying Jaclyn's face with apprehension, as though anticipating some command, but Jaclyn wasn't looking at him.

"What are you going to do?" Jaclyn returned Jordan's questions with one of her own.

"I don't know what you mean."

Jaclyn came out from behind the desk and there was a moment where Jordan's eyes skimmed the map there. Small lumps of rock had been placed strategically throughout the terrain, some over blue, some over brown and green. Then Jaclyn's body blocked the view. She covered half the distance to Jordan, mother and daughter were now facing each other, brown and teal eyes clashing.

Jaclyn spoke slowly. "I mean, now that you know what you are, and where I am…what are you going to do?"

Jordan exhaled a breath full of irony and disbelief. "I thought you would come with me to Rodania. And we could go home together, to Virginia. We could get Dad, and—"

"And what?" Jaclyn cocked a perfectly manicured brow. "Live happily ever after?" Her voice dropped to a whisper. "So foolish." She closed the rest of the distance between them and stopped no less than a foot from Jordan; they were nose to perfect nose. Jaclyn raised her hand slowly. Her fingers closed around a lock of blonde hair at Jordan's temple. She tucked it almost lovingly behind Jordan's ear. Then she laid her hand on Jordan's cheek with her thumb wrapped over Jordan's jaw. Her touch was soft, but Jordan had the fleeting impression of bared teeth and claws. "The way I see it…" Jaclyn tilted Jordan's face up to the light. "My beautiful girl, is that you have no choice."

Jordan's brows drew together as she stared into Jaclyn's eyes. Fear began to climb hand over claw up her ribcage, like a gargoyle made of ice.

"I am in charge here, as I'm sure you've noticed. This island is my throne. Nothing happens in Maticaw that I don't know about. Nothing happens in Operyn or Skillen that I don't know about. Soon I'll operate the ports of Jegriar and Comipyr, too. After that…" Jaclyn shrugged. "We shall see what comes next."

Jordan's mind was racing like an out of control thoroughbred, imaginary hooves spewing clods of thought in all directions. *What is she talking about?*

"I need someone unassuming, someone innocuous. Someone in Rodania." Jaclyn released Jordan's face and held both hands out. "And here you are." She smiled.

It was a perfect smile on a perfect mouth, revealing perfect teeth. So why did Jordan feel like she was standing in front of a cobra with its hood spread wide and its fangs bared in a hiss? Jordan took a step back.

Sol's words materialized in Jordan's memory. *Seems the new trade-master at Maticaw, some fellow by the name of Jack, is putting up roadblocks.*

"Jack," Jordan whispered, her eyes widening. "Jaclyn." She inhaled. "You're Jack! You're the one bungling up the trade of that medicine—" Jordan floundered for the name of it, but it wasn't important. "Why are you denying sick people their medicine?"

Jaclyn frowned and looked bored. "Altruistic, just like your father." She returned to the desk. "You can stay with Stefania, my secretary, until I figure out what to do with you." Her tone was finite, as though Jordan had no say in the matter.

Jordan took another step backward, feeling the walls closing in. Her heart was pounding, and her eyes skimmed the stone walls for a window she might have missed somehow.

I need air.

Jaclyn looked up and watched Jordan walk backward until her back bumped the door. Jordan's hand found the handle behind her.

"Where do you think you're going?" Jaclyn propped a fist on her hip.

Jordan's temples throbbed and she felt as though strong, cold hands were choking her. She reached up to her neck, but there was nothing there. Her eyes flashed to the silver locket on the desk where Jaclyn had set it down. The scene before her blurred and Jordan felt a wave of nausea roll her stomach into itself. She couldn't breathe. Wet drops spilled down her cheek and off her chin.

I'm having a panic attack, she realized. *That's what this is.* She pulled at the neck of her vest, but it was loose. *I'm going to suffocate!* It was too much: the harpy attack, the shock and disappointment of finally finding Jaclyn and realizing she was not what Jordan had been imagining her entire life. Jordan gasped for air, whirled, and yanked on the door, bolting from the room.

Jaclyn watched the door thump shut behind her daughter.

"What a coward. As if she'd be any good to me, anyway."

"You want me to go after her?" Ashley watched Jaclyn's face. Years in her service and he still couldn't tell what the woman was thinking. *I doubt I ever will. Jaclyn is the most unpredictable person I've ever known.*

"Yes, Ash." Jaclyn said softly.

Ashley needed more than that. "Want me to take her to Stefania's? She can't go back to Rodania; not with what she knows."

"No, she can't." Jaclyn meditated, chewing her lip. "If she's not with us, she is against us. Blood or no." She paused; then, "Finish her." She spoke plainly, like she was ordering something for breakfast.

Ashley's face paled at this directive. "Are you sure?" His voice was hoarse. *I have done many distasteful things under Jaclyn's charge over the years, but murder an innocent girl? Jaclyn's own daughter?*

Jaclyn turned her head slowly and nailed the Arpak with a look that said she wouldn't repeat herself.

Mutely, he nodded. With his mouth in a grim line and dread in his young breast, Ashley crossed the carpet on silent feet and left the office.

CHAPTER 20

Jordan was nearly blind with tears as she ran through the lobby and past the secretary's desk. She couldn't see well enough to tell if the girl was there or not and there was no one calling out to her to ask her to stop or see if she was okay. Not knowing any other way out but the way she'd come in, Jordan ran down the carpeted hall and turned down the corridor full of paintings. She was gasping for air, her heart was racing. She found the basement door and yanked it open, pounding down the staircase into the dark. She ran straight, past the stored goods. The basement door shut behind her, cutting off her only source of light. Panting and feeling like she might pass out, Jordan reached for the huge wooden door in the dark. She fumbled for the latch, her wings trembling and legs quaking. With a great heave, she pushed the door open and dashed forward, out into driving rain. *When did this storm start?*

Her mouth open and her chest heaving, Jordan turned her face up to the sky, already soaked from the downpour. She gasped and sucked in air like she'd run for her life. She lost her balance and *thump*ed back onto her butt on the hard wet stones. Her palms scraped against grains of sand and her wings thrust out awkwardly to the side in a too-late effort to catch her. She sat there on the cold, wet ground, her clothing and hair soaking through, her face upturned. She sucked in air greedily and, slowly, her heart eased its clatter. The feeling of a fist around her throat dissipated. Her feathers felt heavy, sodden, and she shook her wings. Jordan opened her eyes, blinking against the droplets falling into her face. Distant thunder cracked and lightning flashed over Maticaw. Small circles of light drew Jordan's attention back to the stone fortress. She tilted her head back and looked up at the small line of round windows.

One of the windows darkened as a head appeared, blocking out the light. A face peered out to the blackening sea, scanned sideways, then tilted down. Jordan recognized the shape of the head.

Ashley.

He disappeared.

Jordan scrambled to her feet, knowing as surely as the sea was salty that Ashley was coming after her. Every nerve bellowed that she should not wait to find out what he wanted.

"Blue!" Jordan screamed as she bolted across the beach toward the water. Her boots pounded on the rock slabs, and her wings opened. She took to the air, calling for her dragon, her voice rough and on the edge of panic. "Blue, we have to leave. Now!" Her wings beat and worked, taking her high above the crashing waves. Twinkling lights in the distance was all the light Jordan could see. The moving lights would be ships sailing in and out of the harbor; the still lights would be those of Maticaw. Jordan tucked her arms in tight, squeezed her legs tight together the way Sol had shown her, and flew as hard as she had earlier that day. Wet blackness swallowed her and rain pelted her face. She closed her nictitating membranes and her vision cleared as the lid protected her eyes.

"Blue!" She called again. Then she realized that if Ashley were on her trail, she'd be giving him a beacon that would lead him right to her. She stopped yelling for Blue but scanned the darkness for her companion, hoping to see his flapping shape materialize from the void. She took a glance back at the island, but saw nothing but a caul of rain and the lights of the trade office growing dim in the distance. White sprays of froth and foam appeared and disappeared as the waves threw themselves suicidally against the stone slabs of the beach.

Her wings ached with heaviness, still she powered her way forward, mentally begging Blue to follow her. She glanced back again just as lightning forked across the sky.

Her heart scrambled into her throat.

A winged form, lit momentarily by the flash of light, was not far behind. His wings pounded the air smoothly in spite of the rain, frightening in their capable, unstoppable rhythm. He moved like a starving shark and he was gaining. Lightning flashed again. His dark eyes and lean, square jaw were limned with the fluorescent light. Ashley's expression was terrible, monstrous with intent.

Alarmed, Jordan cried out and doubled her efforts. The lights of Maticaw were growing closer, just not fast enough. She felt like she was in a dream where she was running through sucking mud that hampered her legs and feet, frustrating all her efforts to escape.

The lights from a tall-masted ship floated in front of her vision. Over the open ocean in a rainstorm, with nothing to protect her, there was no way Jordan could combat Ashley and win. The man was formidable; his driving wingstrokes told her all she needed to know about his capabilities. The ships were her only hope. Jordan clenched her teeth and ignored the burning in her wings and lungs. Her skin prickled with the expectation that at any moment she would feel strong hands lock tightly around her ankles. They would yank her backward and hurl her into the water, or perhaps drag her back to the island.

The ship's masts loomed; the sails were white ghosts rising

out of the black. Small shapes ran the decks and rope ladders, working to steady the ship and sail her into the safety of the harbor. Jordan stole a glance back and a scream of terror ripped from her throat. Ashley was so close she could see the mole at his temple and the square shape of his fingernails as a hand reached for her like a claw reaching out from a nightmare.

Praying silently, Jordan turned sideways, reached out both hands and hooked them on the mast of the ship as she sped by it. The face of a young boy in the ship's crow's nest gaped up at her and watched her use the mast as an axle. Her body jerked around violently, splinters biting into the skin of her hands. Her shoulders jerked painfully in their sockets. The mast tore from her grip as Ashley went sailing by, buying her only moments.

There were shouts from the sailors below. Jordan ignored them, putting all her efforts into using the momentum of her abrupt turn to shoot for the docks of Maticaw. Surely Ashley would not pursue her there, where they'd be observed. Her hands bleeding and her shoulders and wrists throbbing, Jordan spiralled and dove low to fly over the waves, hoping to use the increasing number of ships as cover. She looked back and saw Ashley take a banking turn and disappear behind the sails of the ship. He was far more agile than a harpy. Jordan could hardly believe that she was flying so hard for her life for the second time that day. If she had been fresh, maybe she could have evaded her pursuer with more ease, but she was already tired from her earlier sprint.

Skimming so low over the water that she received rude, wet slaps in the face, Jordan felt her wingtips touch the water's surface. She swerved between two vessels as they passed one another, the port lights growing bright and blinding her momentarily. She banked toward Maticaw; the pocket of civilization with two jutting peninsulas opening their arms to welcome Jordan.

A hand clamped around Jordan's right calf. Jordan squealed

and shook her leg violently. She looked back at Ashley, and their eyes clashed. His face was red, and a vein throbbed in his temple. His wings flexed, changing angles, and with his powerful backstroke, Jordan felt her momentum slow. He reached his other hand out for her other leg. She jerked it away from him and sent her booted foot into his face. She only half connected with his jaw, but the glancing blow made him grunt, and his grip loosened.

She faced front just as the massive prow of a ship sliced toward them in the water. Spray flew out to either side as the hull smashed down on the sea. There was no time to scream. Jordan rolled over onto her back, yanking her arms to her chest and her left wing out of the ship's path; the wooden hull sliced by, like a hammer swung through the water by some giant. Ashley's hand released her calf as he broke from her, toward the other side of the ship. Jordan thought she heard a *thump* as a body part bounced off the hull. She fought to right herself and hoped that Ashley would be at least temporarily incapacitated. Exhaustion throbbed in her oxygen-starved muscles and she sucked in breath after breath, her throat burning. Catching a faceful of seawater, she spluttered and coughed and fought to clear her vision and climb higher at the same time.

Ashley appeared below her, skimming the waves. He was clutching one arm to his chest and craning his neck to find her. His eyes locked on to his prey and he carved toward her with a terrifyingly sharp turn.

Her wings aching and her lungs blistering, Jordan gritted her teeth and begged her pinions for more speed and power. She was flagging badly and she knew it. But Maticaw was so close now. Her hand drifted to the hilt of the remaining blade Sol had given her. *Am I going to have to face Ashley in combat?* He'd made his intentions clear—capture Jordan at any cost. She didn't think from his expression that he was planning to put her up in a suite and feed her an eight-course dinner. Every sense she had was screaming at her that her life was in danger. There was no time to luxuriate in the shock that Ashley was acting on her mother's orders. It was a realization that lingered at the sides of Jordan's consciousness, refusing at this time to step into the light.

Maticaw's port loomed out toward them like giant fingers stretching out to sea as the Arpaks swerved between vessels. Jordan made a valiant effort to pull her legs forward the way Sol had shown her and catch herself on a dock in a run, but her muscles seized as her feet hit the nearest platform. Her legs gave out and she tumbled forward off the edge of the dock and into the waves. Icy water closed over her head, stabbing her skin and filling her clothing and boots. Her sodden wings became heavy ballasts and flailed uselessly at the water. Using her arms, Jordan pulled for the surface. Only her face broke through, the driving rain pelting her as she gasped for air.

A voice was calling garbled words she couldn't make out, as her ears were full of water. She sucked in breaths, her chest still near exploding, and looked around.

A creature, a sort of man with all the appropriate number of limbs and eyes, but with a mouth far too big for his face, was kneeling at the edge of the dock and reaching a hand out to her. He yelled words at her, punctuated by what could only be called chirps and squeaks. It didn't matter that she couldn't understand him, his intention was clearly to help her out of the water. In his ghastly face was a welcome concern, so Jordan reached for him.

The two of them strained toward each other, Jordan paddling furiously with one hand and kicking for all she was worth with her lead-filled boots.

The rain on Jordan momentarily stopped as a shadow fell over her. The creature on the dock looked up and surprise widened his eyes. His massive mouth dropped open, looking like a cave full of blunt teeth. More of those strange words poured out, sounding indignant now.

Strong hands grabbed Jordan by the back of her vest and belt and she was heaved up out of the water like she was little more than a child's toy. The sharp snaps of wet but strong wings pounded over her head. Jordan craned her neck to look behind her. Ashley had lifted her straight out of the water and was carrying her over the docks. The creature that had tried to help her sailed by below; his hand was still outstretched, his huge mouth gaping.

"Let me go!" Jordan tried to scream, but the words barely came out. It was all she could do to breathe. She tried to lift her wings but they felt like they were made of sod—impossibly heavy, nothing more than a prop to weigh her down. The muscles in her back and shoulders strained with effort. *If I can muster enough energy to shake the water off, I might have a chance.* She clenched her teeth and tried, but her wings just quivered and cried out for rest.

Ashley carried her over the docks and past the beach, where the sea cradled the coast. The port of Maticaw and the safety of its civilization, was far behind them now. Below them was a shield of mossy rocks and scrubby trees. The branches of the gnarly trees all reached back toward the forest, looking for all the world like they'd been trying for years to get off the windy, barren coast.

Jordan heard the sound of a blade being drawn. Terror fueled her body and she clenched her jaw so tight it was surprising she didn't crack any molars. Using every ounce of energy she had, she jerked sideways into a barrel roll. Ashley's grip on her clothing broke. One of her sodden wings slapped across his face and chest, knocking him sideways.

Jordan gasped as the sensation of falling clutched at her stomach. Pain burst through the back of her head and streams of fire scraped along her spine and the arches of her wings as she hit the rocks and skid, her legs flipping once over her head. She slammed up against a tree and received a hard poke in the back. Jordan wanted nothing more than to lie still and wait for the pain to pass, but the sound of boots running along rock screamed at her to rise.

Her bruised and scraped body hurt with every breath, she suspected she might have lost some of the feathers on the tops of her wings, for they burned with a searing pain.

She disentangled herself from the tree, stretching her wings out wide to feel if they still worked. As she got to her shaky legs and straightened, a fresh sheet of rain swept across the rocks. A form materialized through the driving drops. Ashley was striding toward her, a long two-sided blade in one hand.

He's going to kill me. Jordan's hand fumbled for her own knife, and she yanked it free of its sheath. Her wrist throbbed and her fingers felt numb; she could barely feel the blade, and she sure couldn't clench it tight. She held the blade out in front of her, shaking. Water ran over her face and down the back of her neck. Her hair hung down into her eyes and stuck to her cheeks, and she thrust it back with her free hand.

Ashley raised his blade, almost upon her.

Time slowed and Jordan clearly saw the man's eyes, his expression. He was going to kill her, but there was a repugnance in his eyes—like he was dreading ending her life. Perhaps that was something she could use.

"Ashley," Jordan cried out, the knife quivered in her loose grip. "Please, don't do this!"

"I *have* to," he answered immediately, his voice full of passion and torment. "I'm sorry."

"No, you don't." She staggered backward as he advanced, knowing she'd be dead before they even crossed steel. "I'll go away and never come back."

He actually seemed to consider this, but in the span of the same breath, he rejected it. "Don't make this harder," he gritted out. He reached out to grab her. "I'll make it quick."

Jordan stumbled and fell back on her tailbone. When she tried to get to her feet, her legs refused to obey. She faced her attacker, holding her blade up.

Ashley loomed over, blade raised.

A small silver thing appeared in the flesh of his shoulder. Ashley looked down at the blade protruding from his skin. He didn't cry out in pain or stumble back screaming; just looked at the knife, trying to work out how it had gotten there. Blood blossomed around the blade like a flower in the fabric of his soaking shirt.

Jordan looked into the dark, scrubby brush and in the crevices of the rock slabs, expecting to see that Sol had magically finished his delivery in record time and come to find her.

But the broad mercenary that materialized from the shadows like a wraith, his great wings tucked tightly behind him, and his dewclaws framing his face, was not Sol.

"Toth!" Jordan cried out, never so happy to see anyone in her life as she was to see the Nycht mercenary. She crawled out from under Ashley's reach as the Arpak straightened, lifting his hand to pluck the blade from his shoulder. Blood was now streaming from the wound down his arm. Ashley tossed the blade onto the stones, where it made a wet pinging tumble.

Toth reached Jordan and bent to help her up.

"Why are you always in trouble?" he asked, keeping his eyes on Ashley, who had just unsheathed a second blade. The expression on Ashley's face was one of weary annoyance. Instead of making one easy kill, he now had to make two, and the second one didn't look like it was going to come easy.

"That's a fair question," panted Jordan, standing on her own two feet and bubbling over with relief. "If we live through this, will you please teach me how to fight?"

Toth's brows shot up. " 'If'?" His eyes, dark in the dim light of the rainstorm, darted to Jordan's face and then back to Ashley, who was pacing in the distance as though waiting for their duel to begin. "You have doubts?" Toth unhitched a loop of chain from his waist and held it out from his body. A spiked iron ball dangled from the end. He began to swing it to and fro.

"No." Jordan gulped. "But do you think we could just let him go?" It didn't matter that Ashley had scared the living crap out of her, or that her body was aching from top to toe. Relief at being rescued filled her with generosity. She didn't want to see anyone's blood spilled, even Ashley's.

"That depends on him," Toth replied. The spiked ball began making deadly circles at his side. Toth's eyes were locked on Ashley.

Ashley tucked his chin down and glowered. He sheathed one of the blades and reached behind his head to retrieve the axe fastened to his back that Jordan had no idea was even there.

Jordan's hands flew to her face. "Oh, this isn't good."

"I'll meet you at a pub in Maticaw called *The Silver Pony*," said Toth quietly. "Go on. You don't want to watch this."

"I'm not leaving you!" Jordan shouted. "Are you nuts?"

"Jordan—"

The rest of Toth's sentence was swallowed up by a roar so loud, it made Jordan clap her hands over her ears.

Blue dropped out of the sky and landed on the rock in between Toth and Ashley, his head down low and his wings spread wide. The reptile was small, but with his teeth bared and his eyes alight with fury, he was terrible to behold. He made an awful hissing rattle and took a few steps toward Ashley, his back to Toth and Jordan. His body language said that Ashley was soon to be barbecue. Blue was making those same strange sounds he had made before he'd roasted the harpy earlier that day.

Toth put an arm across Jordan and pushed her back behind him, his body tense and half-crouched. "Dragon?" Toth hissed in surprise.

"It's Blue!" Jordan yelled, slapping her palm on Toth's shoulder rapidly and repeatedly with excitement. "He's mine!"

Toth gaped. "That thing is with you?"

Jordan nodded and grinned like a fool, still so relieved that today was not the day she would meet her maker. "He's really sweet—"

Blue roared again, and a long tongue of hot flames jetted from his mouth. The fire consumed a nearby tree and licked out towards Ashley. The Arpak staggered back, his eyes squinting in the light; he threw a forearm up against the heat. A line of small fires crackled and hissed under the rain, sputtering out. Spirals of steam drifted up from the smoking trail leading away from the dragon as the rain beaded and ran down Blue's scales.

Jordan's eyes adjusted after the bright burst of light, searching for Ashley. Her predator was nothing but a faint, flying form in the distance.

CHAPTER 21

The two Strix barely spoke after Ashley had flown away. Jordan's joy at being rescued (again) by Toth was soon replaced by shock. The first order of business was getting dry and fed, and dressing Jordan's wounds. She had abrasions on the back of her head and the tops of her wings. Every muscle in her body had begun to stiffen. Toth half-carried Jordan through the streets with a supporting arm under her wings, hooked around her ribcage. With the rain driving down on them, and Blue flying overhead and screaming (almost laughing) about how easy it had been to scare away that Arpak, Toth led Jordan to a hideaway tavern. Located on a side street just off the boardwalk and with a very small, easy-to-miss sign, *The Silver Pony* was warm and cozy and smelled of stew, wet wool, and damp leather. They'd collapsed at a table. Blue had curled up underneath it, snugged against Jordan's feet.

Jordan and Toth now sat hunched over two gigantic bowls of goulash in the dim yellow light of the tavern. Jordan's hands were both bound with bandages, after Toth had patiently plucked multiple slivers from her tender flesh and tied up the bandages in a way that allowed her to use her fingers. Her body still trembled from the chase and she dropped her spoon several times. Toth shot her concerned glances but didn't say anything about her quaking hands.

"Where did you get the dragon?" Toth asked after he'd finished his bowl of food and pushed it aside.

"Accidentally," Jordan said, her eyelids drooping. "He imprinted on me the last time I was in Maticaw."

Toth grunted. He knew about dragon imprinting. It was rare, but it happened. His eyes trailed to the wings arching over Jordan's head.

"Nice wings."

Jordan's eyes flashed to his face. "I didn't know. The Elves that helped Sol told me I was an Arpak descendant." Jordan took another slow bite of food. The muscles in her shoulder creaked as she lifted the spoon.

"Bit of a surprise for you?"

Jordan almost spat out her mouthful of goulash as she laughed. "That's the understatement of the century," she said around her food. She put down her spoon, swallowed and wiped her mouth. "What are you doing here? How did you know I was in trouble? The Conca is miles from here. Don't get me wrong, I'm thrilled." Her eyes met his. "I'd be a corpse by now, if it weren't for you."

"I didn't know you were in trouble," Toth replied, lacing his fingers on the table. His eyes darted about the dim tavern, scoping out the patrons, watching for Ashley or any strangers discreetly, or not so discreetly observing them. But *The Silver Pony* was benign and sleepy on this stormy night. Patrons were draping wet clothing out in front of the fire and hanging soaked hats on the hooks before tucking into a meal. Friendly conversation and laughter provided pleasant background noise, covering up Toth and Jordan's conversation. "Your friend Eohne came to visit me."

Jordan straightened with surprise and then winced as the

movement sent shooting pains down the muscles on either side of her spine. "Eohne? You know her?"

"I do now." Toth looked at Jordan thoughtfully, weighing his next words. *If I tell Jordan that her father is in trouble, she'll want to go running after him immediately. After what she's been through, she is in no shape to go anywhere tonight. Then again, if I wait to tell her, she'll be upset with me for it.* Toth decided he could handle Jordan's anger.

"How did *she* know I was in trouble?" Jordan took another slow bite. "Elf magic?"

"Something like that," was Toth's cryptic reply. "I'm going to see about getting a room." Jordan opened her mouth to ask him to explain further but he was already gone, striding toward the bar. He leaned an elbow on the counter and began to talk with the bartender.

Blue's nose hooked under Jordan's ankle and he propped up her bare foot with his head. Jordan's boots and socks were drying by the fire. Jordan peered under the table into the gloom. Blue's shining eyes stared up at her from under her ankle. He somehow gave off the impression of remorse.

"It's alright, Blue." Jordan reached her fingers down to stroke his nose. "You saved me." Jordan felt eyes on her and looked up to catch Toth staring at her from the bar and frowning. He looked away. "You and Toth both did," she amended. She went back to her meal and put away the rest of her goulash.

With her stomach full and without Toth to distract her, Jordan's mind drifted to her meeting with Jaclyn. None of it made much sense. *Why would Jaclyn send her mercenary to kill her own daughter? Was the fact that she was masquerading as 'Jack' a critical enough secret to end an innocent woman's life over?* The predacious way Jaclyn had analyzed Jordan's face, the way those calculating brown eyes had swept her with cool detachment, made Jordan shiver. She scraped her damp hair back from her face and realized that her face was wet with tears. She rubbed the moisture away and took a steadying breath. She wished again for Sol's presence.

Toth returned to the table and sat across from her. "Are you going to tell me who that was and why he wanted to kill you?" He rested his forearms on the table and leaned forward, all ears.

"His name is Ashley," Jordan answered, wiping another errant tear from her cheek. "He works for my mother, that's all I know about him."

"Your…" Toth's eyes clouded with unease. "Your mother? You found her, then?"

"I found her."

"And?"

"And she sent her guard to kill me."

"I've gathered that. Why?" Toth lay his palms up on the table.

"I have no idea." Jordan sniffed. Her nose had begun to tingle. "All my life I've been told what a sweet, kind-hearted woman my mother was. When she disappeared, my father poured every resource into finding her. She never left a note or any other clue about where she'd gone or why. All this time, I—" Jordan cleared her throat, which was beginning to feel scratchy. She took a drink of water from her cup. "I thought maybe she'd been taken, or she was in some kind of trouble. There had to be a good explanation for why and how she left."

Toth waited while Jordan blew her nose into her napkin. Jordan's voice was growing raspy, stuffed up sounding.

Jordan shook her head, a harsh line formed between her brows. "So my mother is a b-bitch." Another hot tear tracked its way to her chin. She hiccoughed and brushed it off with the kerchief, the movement full of annoyance. "I won't fall apart for her," she said fiercely, tucking the kerchief away. She gave three violent sneezes in a row, and Blue was up on the bench in a flash, his chin in her lap. She pulled the kerchief out again.

"I'm glad to hear it," praised Toth, feeling like he was watching a hand-knit sweater unravel before his eyes. "But you might fall apart if we don't get you to bed. You can tell me the rest of the story tomorrow. Come on. I've got you a room."

Jordan got to her feet, wincing at the stiffness gathering in her muscles. "Feels like rigor mortis," she muttered.

Toth went to the fire and gathered up their wet things. Draping them over his arm, he returned to the table, pulling a key from a pocket in his vest.

"What about you?" asked Jordan, swaying unsteadily. Her head had begun to pound.

"Don't worry about me. I'm nocturnal. I'm going to do a bit of scouting while you sleep. If I'm right," Toth said, eyeballing her red nose and puffy eyes, "you'll sleep until noon. I'll catch some sleep in the morning."

Jordan was too tired to protest. She followed Toth to the rear of the tavern, where they pushed outside and crossed an open courtyard. The rain had thinned to a light shower and dusted their hair with tiny beads. Blue ambled behind Jordan, keeping so close to her that he nearly tripped her.

Toth unlocked one of three doors clustered together like a fleur-de-lis. They entered a cozy, whitewashed room with a double bed, two chairs, a water pitcher and bowl, and a small fire crackling in a hearth at the corner. A single window was open a crack, the evening's breeze drifted through the room as the door opened.

Toth pulled the chairs so their backs were to the fire and draped their things over them to continue drying. "Get some sleep. I'll be back to check on you."

"But you…" Jordan stood in her bare feet in the middle of the room. She was so tired she could barely talk. She felt like doing nothing more than crawling under the covers and crying herself to sleep.

Blue crawled underneath one of the chairs, lay down on his tummy and peered out at them.

"Use this to dry off," Toth picked up a towel hanging on a

hook near the water pitcher and handed it to her. "I'll see if I can find some medicine for you."

"Medicine? I'm not sick," Jordan replied hoarsely.

Toth gave a half smile. "You're well on your way."

"Do you know Cles, too?" Jordan put a hand to her temple.

Toth cocked his head. "Cles?"

"The apothecary. I never met him, but I remembered his name when Sol told me—"

"Jordan?"

"Hmmmm?" Her eyes drifted half closed. Her voice sounded like it was coming from between her eyes.

Toth put his hands on her shoulders and walked her backward until she had no choice but to sit on the bed. "Sleep now. We'll talk tomorrow."

"Okay," Jordan sighed, gazing at the pillow beside her with a dopy expression.

Toth let himself out of the room and locked the door behind him.

* * *

Toth stepped out into the cool, drippy evening. He passed back through *The Silver Pony* and made his way down the alley toward the docks. Mist had gathered fast on the streets of Maticaw after the rain had cleared. Droplets fell from lampposts and smeared dimly lit windows. The sounds of restless waves breaking on rocks filled the lower half of Maticaw. Dim lights from sailing vessels docked in port glowed with misty rings around them. Visibility closed in to a mere city block and shapes drifted in and out of the fog as people walked by—some of them greeting Toth as they passed.

Fog didn't bother Toth. He was a creature built for the night and was even armed to deal with pitch-black, or blindness, if he had to. All Nychts were equipped with a secondary voice box capable of high-frequency sound output and ears able to detect sounds much too high-pitched for human ears. But Toth wasn't in need of sound waves on this particular night; he was more concerned about remembering how to use the little glass balls Eohne had given him to send a message to the Elf that he'd found Jordan.

"Get to high ground," Toth muttered, recalling step one. "These things better work in foggy weather." Magical tools made Toth uneasy.

Toth made his way to the end of the dock and took a flying jump from the rocks at the waters edge. His wings snapped out and he pulled for the sky, heading away from the water and toward the higher streets of the city. Below him, the fog swirled as his wings cycloned the air. Maticaw's lights became blurred clusters of faerie lights in dark alleys. The fog thinned as he climbed and now the city was made of towers and spires poking up through the mist. He made for a distant hilltop illuminated by the barely visible moons; *a park*, he assumed. He landed on the wet grass, his boots sliding over the uneven surface. There was nothing about Maticaw that was straight; the entire city was built on craggy steps of rock.

He fumbled in his bag for the jar Eohne had given him, and held his find up in the moonlight. She'd given him twelve of the strange bugs. She'd mentioned that the Elven princess didn't really want them used, but Eohne felt they had no choice. Toth hoped some Elven magic didn't cleave him when he used them. He dubiously eyed the little pill Eohne had given him. Shrugging, he tossed it into his mouth. *Here goes nothing.*

Eohne had warned him about the choking sensation but it still took him by surprise. His hand flew to his neck as he said the words he needed to say; the sounds stopped up in his throat and expanded there. The urge to cough was nearly unbearable. The bean slid back up his throat and onto his tongue, and he spat it into his hand with a sound of disgust. "*Eurgh*. Elf magic." Toth was much more a fan of principles he could understand: gravity, wind, a beating heart, a sharp blade clutched in his fist—things like that.

Toth put the bean in the water the way Eohne had instructed and watched while it changed color. He pulled the fluid into the syringe and injected it one by one into the messenger bugs, leaving them to hang in the air above his head. The balls were small and slippery in his hardened fingers and he dropped more than one of them in the process. If he hadn't had extraordinary night vision, he'd have fumbled around in the wet grass in the dark for a long time trying to locate the clear balls.

Doubt that this strange magic would even work wormed its way into Toth's heart as he injected the bright green fluid into each glass ball. *What if it fails? How will we find each other then? What if these stupid little balls don't like me for some reason?* He shoved the doubts aside—he'd find out momentarily if someone other than an Elf could do Elf magic.

Toth barked the commands and the message for Eohne, including that he'd found Jordan and gave the location of *The Silver Pony*. With his closing command, the balls zipped off toward the water so quickly they were nothing but a green blur. *So much for not working.* Toth stood there looking out toward Rodania and beyond that, Trevilsom, for a long time.

CHAPTER 22

Allan turned his face toward the door of his small wooden cell as a key jingled in the lock. His neck spasmed and he reached up a hand to rub at the ache. The box wasn't nearly high enough to accommodate Allan's full height, the most comfortable posture he'd been able to find was sitting with his back against the wall so his neck could be straight, or curled into a fetal position. *If I don't get to straighten my legs soon, I will go completely insane.*

Allan had been tortured by Marceau's directive to 'Retarder le navire.' It was simply impossible. Faking illness had been his only idea and, as it turned out, he didn't have to fake it. The seasickness was unrelenting; his captors were unmoved by it.

The short, heavy, wooden door of his cell swung open on squeaky hinges. Allan closed his eyes against the bright light that streamed in and assaulted his eyes. The squat, lumpy shape of a being who smelled like moldy vegetables blocked out some of that light. Foreign words were grunted at him, but with the addition of helpful gestures so that Allan was able to work out the meaning: 'come out of the box, and be quick about it.'

Allan went to his hands and knees and crawled forward,

ducking his head to fit through the doorway of the box he'd been living in while the ship crossed a turbulent ocean. His captors had been kind enough to find a pail for him to be sick in and had even taken it away to wash it out. They'd also provided him with a bucket of drinking water. *How thoughtful.* The hold of the ship stank of rot; even if he hadn't been seasick, it was enough to make a person ill.

He'd finally grown accustomed to the smell and didn't even notice it anymore. Eight holes punched in the ceiling had let in stale air and a muted light, as though the box was inside another box with more windows.

Allan's back protested as he straightened for the first time in days. His stomach clenched as the ship lurched under his feet and he could feel from the concave shape of his abdomen that he'd lost weight. *How could I not? Being too seasick to eat and too stressed to think of anything but Jordan and how to get out of this mess, how to find her...*

The lump of a creature in front of him wrapped a rope haphazardly over his wrists, which tightened as if by magic and held his hands lashed in front of him. The lump grouched at him, shoving Allan forward through the hull of the ship. The hold was full of crates and barrels, trunks and strange-looking cylinders. Looking back, Allan saw that his cell was indeed a box inside a box, one of only two of a kind. The other held no prisoner, as far as he could tell.

Up the stairs Allan lurched, his stomach swaying and his mouth watering. He climbed to the next deck; a just-as-disorganized sleeping quarters. Hammocks swayed and bottles rolled across the floor as the ship lurched. The square main hatch lay open to the sky and salt spray dripped from the underside of the hatch door. Prodded in the ribs by his grumpy escort, Allan staggered his way up the steps to the main deck and into the sea air. Breathing deeply, Allan almost sighed with pleasure as his brain fog cleared. He caught a glimpse of tall, jagged stones jutting up from the churning sea on either side of the small sailing vessel.

Peering toward the helm and squinting in the light, Allan spotted the man behind the wheel—or woman, rather. She was swathed in red fabric from head to toe, including a turban that kept her hair off her face. She was also squat and lumpy, and Allan suspected she might share some DNA with his escort. She steered the small ship through the dragon's teeth of dangerous rocks like she'd navigated it a thousand times before. The crew crawled over the ship like ants, tending to the sails and ropes and shouting foreign words from the crow's nest. Allan had come to think of them as walking turnips, since they were all broad at the shoulders, lumpy, pale, and covered in pallid rough skin the color of autumn leaves. They had a sickly sweet scent and carried short, serrated daggers—which he'd become acquainted with, as they had been waved menacingly in his face more than once.

Allan was allowed to stand by the railing and observe the unusual terrain. A thin mist floated above the water's boiling surface and swirled around the jutting stones. In the distance, a dark shadow loomed. Allan swallowed hard as the toothy island ahead grew close. *Is this Trevilsom, the prison the warden at Vischer spoke so proudly of? It has to be; why else would they remove me from my box?*

The dragon's teeth stones appeared on either side of the ship, making the way clear. A dock materialized from the fog: a dark slab of rock with a wooden ladder coated in black slime disappearing beneath the surface. Allan shuddered and attempted to wrap his arms around himself. *Oh, Jordan,* he lamented. *Will I ever see you again?* The ship slowed to a crawl and then, creaking, to a stop. A chain rattled as the anchor was let down.

Allan was jostled and shoved toward the side of the ship, where a rowboat had been lowered into the choppy black seas. More of those serrated blades than were really necessary were on display. *Remarkable how a common language really isn't necessary to communicate certain things...*

Mutely, Allan did as he was told and began to climb down the rope ladder, hands still bound, and into the dinghy, where one of the turnip men was waiting. Allan had spent the first twenty-four hours trying to talk to these creatures to no avail. They either didn't speak English, or pretended they couldn't. Overwhelming even one of them would have been a near-impossible and pointless exercise, considering how weak, exhausted, and sick Allan had become.

The waiting turnip man gnashed something noisily between gray peg-shaped teeth. He spat a lump of slime over the side of the dingy and watched Allan struggle down the rope ladder with his hands still lashed together. His fingers had lost most of their strength. He felt as weak as a child and marvelled at how quickly the body could break down under duress and lack of sufficient food. He also heard Jordan's voice in his head, admonishing him for not working out and taking better care of himself. *I have something to be grateful for though,* he thought with a kind of sick humor as he took the next slippery step down the rope ladder: *they didn't take my glasses away, and they only have one crack across the left lens.*

Allan's grip weakened halfway down the ladder, and he fell, landing hard and twisting his ankle painfully as he crumpled in a heap on the boat's bottom. The turnip-man that waited for him in the boat gave a cruel laugh at Allan's clumsiness. A second turnip-man dropped into the boat behind Allan, nearly landing on his other leg.

As they rowed him toward the miserable island of doom, Allan thought of Jordan. *Was this what happened to her when she passed through the portal? But then, how did she manage to send me a message?* He supposed the best he could do was hope that she had either been rescued from the desert by much friendlier beings, or that she'd made this journey ahead of him and would be there when he arrived. If that was the case, perhaps together they could find a way to escape.

Allan was rowed expertly and rapidly toward the rocky island's edge. Fingers of fog reached up around the toothy rocks they glided by. Rising up in the distance was a fortress made of dark gray stone. Allan felt his bowels turn to water as the prison neared and a cold bitter wind picked up and blasted against him, making him shiver. All he had for clothing was what he'd been wearing before he stepped through the portal—a tank top, a button-up long-sleeved shirt, dress shoes, and pale denim pants that used to be the color of caramel, but were now dingy and stained.

A tall thin shape moved to meet the dinghy as it approached the stone dock. Allan felt cold fingers of dread trace his spine. The being that materialized from the mist to meet them was a bony giant with no neck. No neck, but a column of dark smoke which billowed from its shoulders and balanced a dark floating head. The giant's features were obscured by the cloud of smoke on which the head hovered. Allan shivered violently at this horrible sight.

The turnip-man in the boat gave another grating chuckle and uttered some nonsensical words at Allan before jerking him to his feet. Leaving Allan's wrists bound, the turnip-man jabbed the point of his serrated blade at the dock. Allan got the message: *'Out of the boat, peon.'*

Allan lost his balance as he stood and the turnip shoved him. A single, despairing word croaked from his lips as he almost tumbled headfirst into the rocky, biting sea.

"Jordan!"

Staggering and swaying, his spine and ribs aching and his fingers and toes numb with cold, Allan set foot on the stone dock. As he stepped onto solid land where the creepy giant waited for him, he wondered, *is this where I'm going to die?*

CHAPTER 23

Jordan woke with a wet face and a head full of cotton. Her first thought, before she had even opened her eyes, was *My mother is a horrible person*. She opened her eyes with great effort, feeling like her ocular cavities were full of gel instead of eyeballs.

A chair covered with clothing blurred and then focused. Movement drew her attention to the other chair, which had been set under the window. A shape occupied the chair—a long, slender shape framed by dark brown ribbons of hair.

Jordan rolled over, rubbing her eyes. She wiped the dampness from her face, baffled at its origin.

"You were crying in your sleep," said a soft, familiar voice.

Jordan gasped. "Eohne?"

The Elf came into proper focus. Jordan bolted upright and then groaned and clenched her eyes shut again as her temples throbbed and the room spun.

A weight depressed the mattress beside her and a warm hand squeezed her shoulder.

"Did you bring some of that dog-water with you?" Jordan croaked. "I feel like garbage." Then Jordan opened her eyes and put her arms around her friend. "Sorry. I don't mean to make demands first thing. I'm so happy to see you." Her voice was nasal and plugged-up sounding. "I would do a proper job of expressing it if my head wasn't full of fluff."

Eohne chuckled and hugged Jordan back. "I can help you with that." She got off the bed and went to where her bag was hanging over the back of the chair. She fished inside for a small vial of purple liquid. The liquid was floating at the top of the vial with air beneath it, rather than the other way around. She took a small needle from a pocket and returned to the bed.

"Where's Toth?" Jordan asked.

"He's sleeping in the next room. He said to wake him when you were up."

"And where's Blue?"

"Is that his name?" Eohne smiled. "I can see why."

A yawn split Jordan's face. "Did you let him out?"

"Yes. I arrived early this morning, before it was even light. He was waiting at the door when I came in. Gave me a bit of a startle, but he must be one smart reptile; he let me in without so much as a growl."

"He is smart, and brave." Jordan eyed the vial and needle suspiciously as the Elf sat down next to her. "What is that?" Then, "Nevermind, I don't want to know."

"Finger, please."

Jordan held out her hands. "Take your pick. I have ten." She gave a violent sneeze into her elbow. "Ugh." She sniffed. "Gross. Ow!"

Eohne squeezed a drop of Jordan's blood until it sat on top of her thumb in a bright red bead. She turned the vial of purple liquid upside down so it ran to the bottom of the glass, removed the cork and put the mouth of the vial over the bead of blood. The blood sat at the mouth of the vial for a moment, quivered there and then flew into the gel as though sucked by a vacuum. Jordan watched this with great interest.

"Did you invent this...whatever it is you're doing?"

"Of course," said Eohne. "I only use my own magic. I don't trust anyone else's." Eohne jabbed her own thumb with the needle next and repeated the process until both drops of blood were mingling with the purple gel. She corked the vial and shook it. The purple substance turned a rich chocolate-brown.

"Why did you take your own blood?" asked Jordan.

"I'm healthy. When you put this gel on the back of your neck where your skull meets your spine, the huriob—that's the liquid—will take my vitality and give it to you."

Jordan looked up at the Elf, horrified. "Will it make you sick?"

Eohne shook her head. "The vitality only travels in one direction. That's the beauty of huriob." She handed the vial to Jordan. "You have to do it, though. If I touch the gel now, the vitality will just go back into me. Be careful not to spill it; if it goes to the ceiling it will be wasted and I don't have time to make more."

Jordan took the vial and turned it upside down. She took off the cork then turned the vial upright while holding her palm over its mouth. The brown liquid ran out of the bottle and hit her cupped hand, where it gathered. She dropped the vial and lifted her hair, rubbing the liquid into the back of her neck where Eohne had said to. "How long does it take to—Whoa!" Jordan straightened. Her whole body tingled from head to toe; her sinuses drained and her eyes cleared. Energy filled her blood and tissue. She flexed her fingers and stared at Eohne. "Is this how you feel all the time?"

Eohne laughed and took the empty vial back. "I guess. Elves don't get sick much." Eohne put the vial back in her bag. "You want to tell me what happened yesterday? Whatever it was, it had you so upset that you were weeping while you slept."

Jordan threw the covers back and got out of bed. Her limbs felt like coiled springs, ready to explode at a moment's notice. She looked down, realizing that she'd slept only in her underwear and the bra Eohne had invented. She cast about for her clothing, remembering that she'd set it by the fire after Toth had left her alone the night before. "I found my mother yesterday."

Eohne frowned. "Toth mentioned that. It didn't go well?"

Jordan picked up her clothing. It was crunchy and stiff. She flexed it to soften it and began to dress. "She was at the Maticaw Trade Office. I guess she runs the place, or something." Jordan sighed miserably. "She tried to have her goon kill me."

Eohne was blinking at her, puzzled. "She *runs* the Trade Office, you say? I thought it was a man who had that job?"

"That's because she's going by the name of Jack instead of Jaclyn. Why? I have no idea." Jordan did up the laces of her pants. "Did you hear me say that she tried to have me killed?"

"It's because that position has always been held by a man," Eohne speculated. "Dealing with sailing captains and shipping crews, many of whom are not as educated as might be ideal, would be tough for a woman. It would be an uphill battle to gain their respect."

"So, what? She never actually faces them in person? Just has some intimidating guy do it for her, while she's behind the scenes, pulling the strings?" Jordan bounced around while pulling on her boot.

Eohne looked thoughtful. "Maybe."

"I did see a tall, mean-looking Arpak leave her office right before I went in. Maybe that was 'Jack'," she made air quotes with her fingers.

"Interesting." Eohne stood looking out the window, where the midmorning sun streamed in across the floor.

"Did I mention she tried to kill me?" Jordan laced up her vest, yanking on the leather thongs with a little more violence than was necessary. She looked down at her hands where there was no pain, remembering that they had been full of slivers. She unravelled the bandages, revealing healthy, pink flesh. She barely felt any amazement. She was getting used to Oriceran's wonders.

"You did." Eohne looked over her shoulder at Jordan, her eyes full of compassion. "I'm sorry, Jordan. I know you were hoping for better."

Jordan barked a laugh. "*Better* than my mother trying to *murder* me?" She put her fists on her hips, her eyes blazing. Now that her burgeoning cold had been nipped in the bud, she was full of razors and bees at the memory of what had transpired the night before. "A hug would have been nice. Maybe some tears of joy." She snatched her blade and sheath off the back of the chair, her movements quick and fiery. "I have to go back there."

Eohne's brows pinched together. "Are you sure that's a good idea?"

Jordan huffed and nodded vigorously. She raised a finger to make a point as to why it was a good idea, then paused. The sound of Ashley unsheathing his blade as he carried her over the rock slabs in the driving rain rang in her memory. Her nod turned into a headshake.

"Nope."

Jordan focused on her friend. The fact that Eohne was standing in front of her, in the flesh, and that Toth was sleeping in the next room, in the flesh, finally sank in. She put her finger down. "What are you *doing* here, Eohne?"

Eohne nodded. "Yes. It's time we had that chat, isn't it?" She moved toward the door. "Let's go wake Toth."

* * *

"You have reason to believe *WHAT?*" Jordan leapt to her feet, knocking the table with her hip and sending their breakfast sliding.

Eohne and Toth snatched at the plates of eggs and feroth bacon and put them back in place. They shared a look that said they had expected a freak out.

Jordan's heart was pounding and her eyes blazed. Her hands flew to her mouth as she muffled a stream of curse words.

"That's why we're here," Toth reminded her. "Sit down. You can't think properly if you're panicking."

Jordan sat like a mechanical doll. "The messenger bugs let him in? That seems like a pretty big design flaw, no?"

Eohne nodded. "It's not part of the desired outcome, certainly."

Jordan put her elbows on the table and dropped her forehead into her hands. "Please tell me you know where he is? Tell me he is okay?"

"I had reason to believe he'd been taken to Vischer. I was there tracking him when Toth found you. Vischer is on the coast, where the Saour Desert meets the Rodanian Sea. It's nothing but an outpost, really."

"And?" Jordan wrung her hands. "I'm guessing he wasn't there, or he'd be with you."

"The gypsies handed him over to a warden. There was probably some sort of sham trial. Wardens get paid to convict, so they tend to…" Eohne tilted her chin down guiltily before she finished her sentence, "fast-track through the formalities."

"And then?" Jordan asked, hoarsely.

"He was put on a ship to Trevilsom."

"Wait, I know that name." Jordan's eyes widened and her throat moved as she swallowed. Sol had mentioned Trevilsom. "It's a prison."

Eohne and Toth both nodded soberly, their eyes glued to her face.

"Are you telling me my father is in some miserable Oriceran *jail*?" The words came out in a horrified whisper.

"Yes, but we're going to get him out." Toth said quietly, putting a hand over Jordan's. Her fingers clutched at his and reached for Eohne's. The three of them clenched hands. Jordan squeezed her eyes shut as her stomach swam. Her breakfast threatened to come up. The warm fingers entwining her own were the only anchors holding her down in a world where she felt otherwise completely adrift.

Jordan felt a big, soft, punching glove full of gratitude thump her in the chest and she opened her eyes, which shone with unshed tears. "That's why you both came? To help me save my dad?" Her lower lip wobbled.

"Of course," said Eohne. She looked uncomfortable and withdrew her hand to shift the straps of her bag to a better place on her shoulder. "I'm at least partially responsible for it happening," she said miserably. "If not fully."

Jordan shook her head. "That's not true. You warned me there were risks."

"Let's focus on next steps," interjected Toth, preferring proactivity to rumination.

Jordan nodded vigorously. "Yes. Okay, so where is Trevilsom?"

Eohne pulled a soft scroll with shredded edges from her bag. She unrolled it and laid it on the table in front of them, using their plates to hold down the edges.

"What, no holographic 3D map?" said Jordan.

"Give me a few weeks, and sure," Eohne replied, looking enthusiastic at the idea. "For now, we have this traditional and ever-trusty paper scroll, which is about a hundred years old and completely out of whack." She laid her hands on the map and peered at it. "But it'll give you a general idea."

Jordan's eyes ran over the image. A curved coastline in the northeast corner showed a large body of water, which was labelled 'Rodanian Sea,' running off the edge of the map. There were several islands scattered throughout, including a three-tiered city titled 'Rodania'. Each point on the map had a hand-drawn icon, such as a kind of fruit, or a pod of leaping fish, or the cartoon heads of beasts. "There's The Conca," Jordan pointed out the long, lightning shaped crevasse on the west side of the map. "Where is your home?" she asked Toth.

"It's not on here. The map is too old for that."

Jordan saw what Eohne meant about the map being out of perspective. The Rodanian islands were much bigger and squatter than the illustration showed.

"Here is Trevilsom," said Toth, pointing a blunt finger directly east of Rodania. The illustration was of sharp, thrusting rocks jutting from the ocean, like some monster's lower jaw, and a figure trapped behind them, bent over and clutching his head with claws for hands.

"Oh, dear," said Jordan, her mouth dry. "How accurate do you think that representation is?"

Eohne and Toth shared a look. "It's probably what you'd expect from a prison," said Eohne.

"Can your magic break him out of there and zap him onto Rodania?"

"It can help," said Eohne, "But I'm afraid it won't be that easy. Trevilsom was built on this island for a reason. It has a magic of its own, which tends to warp foreign magic in unexpected ways." She hesitated. "It also tends to affect the prisoners over time."

"How? What do you mean?" Jordan's eyes roamed her friends face for clues.

"I'm told that it slowly erodes logic, but it affects each species differently, so it's unpredictable."

Jordan stared at Eohne with horror. " *'Erodes logic'*? That sounds like a fancy way of saying that it drives people insane."

"Yes," replied Eohne simply. "But I have reason to believe it doesn't have this affect on humans, only on magical species."

Jordan let out a short sigh of relief. "Well that's a small mercy."

Eohne and Toth shared a look, and Jordan caught it.

"What?" She stared at Eohne.

"It has a different affect on humans."

"For heaven's sake, just spit it out!" Jordan cried. "Stop trying to cushion me and just be honest!"

"It puts them into a sort of coma."

Jordan closed her eyes in horror. Toth's forearms prickled just looking at her.

"Jordan?" Eohne said, gently.

Jordan's teal eyes snapped open. "How much time do we have?"

"We don't know," said Toth, leaning forward. "Trevilsom acts quickly with some inmates and slowly with others. That's why we need to act fast."

"Yes, let's go," barked Jordan, getting to her feet.

"Easy," said Eohne. "We need a plan. We can't just sail into the mouth of the beast without being prepared. We too will be susceptible to Trevilsom's magic if we're not careful."

Jordan sat down, but perched on the edge of her seat. "What do you suggest?"

The two Strix and the Elf bent their heads and began to form a plan, while outside, the sun moved across the sky and the water beat endlessly against ships' hulls.

FINIS

Ascendant is the second book in a four book series. Watch for book three of The Kacy Chronicles: Combatant, this November.

AUTHOR NOTES - A.L. KNORR

WRITTEN SEPTEMBER 3, 2017

So here we are again, clinging to the edge of a cliff, **looks over, nods**. Sorry about this. I didn't actually plan for every installment of The Kacy Chronicles to leave you biting your lip (and possibly flipping me the bird), but sometimes you don't ride art, it rides you. Seems to be the case here, as Jordan, Sol, Allan, Eohne and Toth whisper their story in my ear – I am but a conduit trying to keep up my typing speed. It's funny how stories take on a life of their own. By now these characters seem as real to me as my own friends are, which is a sobering thought. One can only be left hoping that the line between fantasy and reality won't become too blurred. Or maybe its too late for that.

I am assuming, since you're here, reading this, that you made it through both Descendant and Ascendant and you're enjoying the story. WUEEEE, as me and my cohorts in the Oriceran universe have taken to saying. I have ploughed into book 3, which is to be called COMBATANT. I'm sure you'll have some idea of the goings on of this upcoming installment purely on the title alone. Yes, it promises to be an exciting one.

As this universe is growing, I am finding such companionship and camaraderie within the circle of authors, readers, and publishing team. I'm rather over the moon about it. So, thank you for being here, thank you for your emails and messages and reviews. They mean the world to this little writer, pecking away on her laptop (which desperately needs a spray and a q-tip, but I'll spare you the grisly details) in various haunts throughout the world. Today's haunt is the loft of a 1935 craftsman style schoolhouse (recently renovated by said writers parents) in the middle of a windy Canadian prairie. Shortly, I'll be on a plane to Italy, which is where Combatant shall take shape. I hope to catch you on the other side of that story too. Until then...

Thank you to the 'Just-in-time' team of proofreaders, and thank you to the publishing team at LMBPN. Thank you to my beta readers, my street team, my parents and brothers, and to my endlessly supportive circle of friends. I wouldn't be doing this without your magical support. And it is magic, make no mistake. I know magic when I see it.

AUTHOR NOTES - MARTHA CARR

WRITTEN OCTOBER 6, 2017

Some day when I grow up I hope to be just like Abs (that's short for Abby-Lynn or A.L.). Every time I talk to her she's back from a bike ride with friends or taking off for Italy. Or she's mapped out an amazing marketing plan on a spread sheet with costs, dates, places and effectiveness. Frankly, I have a secret envy for anyone who can lay out a pretty spreadsheet. The more complicated the spreadsheet the more I admire you...

On top of all that Abs writes a beautiful, magical and complicated story that draws me in and leaves me wanting more. And Abs manages to do it all without swearing! I may not ever figure that one out...

That's the cool thing about dreams coming true and watching other author's grow into their vision of the good life. There's room for a million different versions and when I see someone blossoming into their dreams, it inspires me to more fully grow into mine. That's reflected in this series full of determination, love and a search for something better that you just know has got to be there. Hang on readers... it's just getting good.

PUBLISHER NOTES - MICHAEL ANDERLE

WRITTEN OCTOBER 5, 2017

Thank you, I cannot express my appreciation enough that not only did you pick up the second book, but you read it all the way to the end and NOW, you're reading these Publisher notes as well.

I have to admit, writing Publisher notes is still (for me) kind of strange. When I dreamt up the Oriceran concepts, and before I reached out to my co-creator Martha Carr on this Universe, I just had a dream.

A dream of something definitely more Urban Fantasy, but with a twist. I wanted to build something where magic wasn't magic, exactly. I wanted it to be a force of energy and a reason for so much of our history that seems to be hinted at by our present archeology digs, but one which mainstream archeologists wave their hands and say, "Nahhh..."

I was raised Southern Baptist, and in the Southern Baptist tradition, there is a LOT of singing in the beginning of the church service. (Which bored my active imagination to tears) and Bible reading. So, whenever I could, I'd skip the singing and read my Bible.

Lot's and LOT'S of Bible reading. *(That's important, here.)*

You see, there is a fair amount in the Old Testament that isn't explained all too well.

For example: If Angels are all around us, why can't we see them?

Now, there are suggestions, but let's make the assumption there are scientific reasons and we start getting to a few interesting potential conclusions.

Such as: Angels exist of light we cannot see (wavelengths we can't see.)

In the Kurtherian Gambit, we talk about how you can create matter (either solid, or gaseous etc.) out of light, which is energy.

Have enough Energy, you have Magic.

Stick this information together, and we can see how scientifically, you could have a being made of light, transform into a corporal (physical) body. Mind you, I haven't figured out the mechanics of the Faith needed to transform from physical to light, but scientifically it is possible to explain this happening.

Here in the Oriceran Universe, we have an energy from the Oriceran world which we have named Magic because we understand that term.

But, is it? Also, we start dealing with the concepts of manipulating this energy to do our will. However, in Martha Carr's book Rule of Magic, we see that Magic can be engaged and allowed to do the best for you, if you let it.

This presumes that Magic has a form of sentience. Now, Martha and I didn't speak on this aspect of creating the magic in Oriceran, so her building it this way was from her own conscious and subconscious. However, I can perceive that we have a very religious text, going back thousands of years, which we can say "See, we aren't that far off of how the Bible talks about this stuff."

If you are willing to just merge what science knows, with those stories over three thousand or more years old we start to wonder…'What if…'

(Don't get me started on the miracles of Moses. We could chat about that for a long time. Remember, the Pharaoh's magicians accomplished mighty feats and you start wondering if they knew something we don't.)

Anyway, all I was trying to do was point out that as a Universe creator, one never knows where the basics of the 'magic' you create comes from. Sometimes, small parts that go to make up the whole come from the places few would suspect.

I hope you enjoy our Universe, and the characters we have created within. It is amazing where the human mind will go, when you allow and encourage it to use the creativity housed between our ears.

Ad Aeternitatem,
Michael Anderle

WANT MORE FROM ORICERAN

JOIN THE EMAIL LIST HERE:

http://oriceran.com/email/
Find the Oriceran Universe on Facebook:
https://www.facebook.com/OriceranUniverse/
Find the Oriceran Universe on Pinterest:
https://www.pinterest.com/lmbpn/pins/

The email list will be a way to share upcoming news and let you know about giveaways and other fun stuff. The Facebook group is a way for us to connect faster – in other words, a chat, plus a way to share new spy tools, ways to keep your information safe, and other cool information and stories. Plus, from time to time I'll share other great indie authors' upcoming worlds of magic and adventure. Signing up for the email list is an easy way to ensure you receive all of the big news and make sure you don't miss any major releases or updates.

Enjoy the new adventure!
    A.L. Knorr and Martha Carr 2017

A.L. KNORR SOCIAL

To be the first to learn about new releases and special offers, sign up for A.L. Knorr's newsletter here: https://www.alknorrbooks.com/

Facebook: https://www.facebook.com/alknorrbooks/
Instagram: https://www.instagram.com/alknorrbooks/?hl=en
Twitter: https://twitter.com/ALKnorrBooks
Pinterest: https://www.pinterest.com/ALKnorrBooks/

MARTHA CARR SOCIAL

Website and Email list: www.marthacarr.com

Facebook Page:
https://www.facebook.com/ChroniclesofLeira/

Facebook Fan Group:
https://www.facebook.com/groups/MarthaCarrFans/

OTHER BOOKS BY A.L. KNORR

Born of Water
(including novella The Wreck of Sybellen)
Born of Fire
Born of Earth
Born of Aether
Born of Air

The Kacy Chronicles
* with Martha Carr *
Descendant (1)
Ascendant (2)
Combatant (3)
Transcendent (4)

Other books and Stories
Pyro (including the novella Heat)
Returning Episode II

OTHER BOOKS BY MARTHA CARR

The Leira Chronicles
* with Michael Anderle *

Waking Magic (1)
Release of Magic (2)
Protection of Magic (3)
Rule of Magic (4)
Dealing in Magic (5)
Theft of Magic (6)
Enemies of Magic (7)
Guardians of Magic (8)

Rewriting Justice
(Leira 2.0)
* with Michael Anderle *
Justice Served Cold (Book 1 May 2018)

I Fear No Evil
* with Michael Anderle *
Kill the Willing (Book 1 May 2018)

School of Necessary Magic
* with Michael Anderle *
Dark is Her Nature (Book 1 May 2018)

The Soul Stone Mage Series

* with Sarah Noffke *

<u>House of Enchanted (1)</u>

The Dark Forest (2)

Mountain of Truth (3)

Land of Terran (4)

New Egypt (5)

Lancothy (6)

Virgo (7)

The Midwest Magic Chronicles

* with Flint Maxwell *

<u>The Midwest Witch (1)</u>

The Midwest Wanderer (2)

The Midwest Whisperer (3)

The Midwest War (4)

The Fairhaven Chronicles

* with S.M. Boyce *

<u>Glow (1)</u>

Shimmer (2)

Ember (3)

Nightfall (4)

ELY PUBLIC LIBRARY
P.O. Box 249
1595 Dows St.
Ely, IA 52227

Made in the USA
Las Vegas, NV
15 January 2022

41420772R00142